Darks A̶̶̶̶̶̶,

Dark Acts

The Redacted Sherlock Holmes

The Novels

Orlando Pearson

Paperback ISBN 978-1-78705-891-0
ePub ISBN 978-1-78705-892-7
PDF ISBN 978-1-78705-893-4

Published by MX Publishing
335 Princess Park Manor, Royal Drive,
London, N11 3GX
www.mxpublishing.co.uk

Cover design Jane Dixon-Smith

Contents

A Summons to Whitehall

Sixty works about my friend, Mr Sherlock Holmes. I have them arrayed before me now as I sit at my desk in this, my ninety-fourth year in November 1947. The British Government asked me to withhold all publication of any further works after 1930. "We do not wish this country's potential foes to know that Sherlock Holmes is still alive, in the same way as we do not confirm the existence of our security services," an official voice said suavely down the telephone to me on the morning of Monday the 7th of July of that year.

By then, the works I had chosen to have published, from the many of which I have records, consisted of no fewer than fifty-six short accounts of cases and four longer ones.

Some have wondered at the imbalance in those numbers.

As does Holmes, who is of the view that there are too many long works.

"Your longer accounts of my cases," opines he, "are prolix. In the short works, and especially in the two where I act as the narrator, I occupy centre-stage almost all the time. In the long ones, either half the work is an explanation of the background to the case, or we are transported to Dartmoor to watch your stumbling efforts at detective work."

"I am obliged," remonstrate I, "to provide a work of the length my publisher has stipulated and to do so, I sometimes need to make my canvas broad."

"But the proportion of that canvas that I occupy is thereby much reduced, and the thrust of my deductive insights correspondingly blunted."

"That, I fear, is the effect of my broadening the canvas."

"My public, may I suggest, good Watson, is far more interested in seeing me work as a detective than in seeing your risible attempts to do so, or in seeing your equally risible attempts to spread a miniature's worth of material across a broad canvas to satisfy the whims of your publisher."

As ever, I was slightly repelled by my friend's egotism, although this reproof meant that I only brought out the broad canvas for the first two accounts of Holmes's cases, which were 'prentice works, for *The Hound of the Baskervilles*, when his public thought Holmes lay drowned at the foot of the Reichenbach Falls, and for *The Valley of Fear*, when my publisher felt an extended read was what was needed to boost morale at the outbreak of the Great War.

So why a long work now?

It is my view that the matters I now relate are of such historic significance that only a work in a longer form will do them justice, and that the public is being sold short if it is permanently deprived of being able to learn of them at whatever point in time the embargo on this work's publication is lifted.

The work's length has the drawback that Holmes, as in my other longer works, is off stage at the *moment critique* of several of its key events, as we – as my reader will discover, I, even more than Holmes – were witnesses at the closest quarters to a game of diplomatic chess that will decide the shape of the world for years, if not decades, to come. And, buried within this game of chess, is the investigation of a multiple murder case which received, for reasons that will become obvious, very little coverage in this country.

In both matters, Holmes displayed complete disregard for his own safety and, if the truth be told, for mine as well. Reckless disregard for the fate of others is a common thread in the narrative that follows, and it is for the reader to decide in each instance whether it was justified. For my own part, I feel that the political ends, which were by and large achieved, were worth this recklessness, but I have no doubt that others will take a different view. My reader may also like to reflect how much choice the chief players in this game of chess actually had – or, indeed whether they were the really the chess players at all, or whether they should, more accurately, be regarded as chess pieces in the hands of forces beyond anyone's control.

I am also proud to note that most of the figures who appear in this work, whether in London, Berlin, Moscow, or in the other locales to which this case took us, show a full knowledge of my friend's published cases. Maybe, after all, there were not so many defects in my choice of which matters to present, or in how I chose to present them.

The events I describe all occurred in the first two years of what is becoming known as the Second World War, yet the case I have described under the title *The Priory School*, which took place in 1903, may perhaps be seen as this narrative's starting point. At the conclusion of that adventure, Lord Holdernesse paid my friend a reward of no less than £12,000 as Holmes recovered his lordship's son, identified the killer of the eponymous school's German master, and remained silent about the criminal involvement of Lord Holdernesse's natural son in the case.

Rendered financially secure by the receipt of this reward, Holmes took the decision largely to withdraw from criminal detective work after this point – certainly, this was the last purely criminal case in which I made any reference to a date, although *His Last Bow*, which was really a matter of state, chronicles events that occurred at the outbreak of the Great War and is dated precisely to August 1914. The motivation behind Holmes's decision to retire from criminal work was to have the most dramatic repercussions, not just on his career as a consulting detective in the first decade of this twentieth century, but far more so in this fifth decade of its calamitous span.

It was in 1937, after the death of my second wife, Jean, that I moved to the Sussex Downs to share, once more, quarters with Holmes. It was there that I had intended to end my days, but in the late summer of 1940, Holmes and I moved to Fenny Stratford in the Buckinghamshire countryside to the west of London. It was to be five years later that I first learned why this village had become our home, when my friend revealed to me his involvement as a consultant with the nearby code-breaking centre at Bletchley Park.

The quiet life of the village quite suited both Holmes and me.

In my old age, I wanted only repose after death had ended each of my two happy marriages. By contrast, I think Holmes's aloofness from the everyday would have rendered him equally capable of being at home or of being apart from normal concerns, anywhere in the world – something which will become more apparent in the variety of scenes in which this work is set.

The rigours of the time brought out the resourcefulness in both of us.

Getting anything to eat beyond bread and potatoes in 1940 – and even those were often in short supply – was such a challenge, that I spent the autumn of that year making a vegetable patch in our garden to plant broad beans and onions, in the hope that would provide us with something to eat in the mid-summer of 1941, when food looked likely to be particularly short. I even experimented with growing tobacco plants, as getting something to fill our pipes with was often as trying as getting something to eat. The same garden also enabled Holmes to carry on his retirement pastime of bee-keeping and most days would find us engrossed in our own affairs.

The evenings saw us at either side of the fireplace, whether we had the coal to keep it lit or not. Inasmuch as we led a life together at all, it was spent trying to remain abreast of the terrible events of the war through newspapers or the wireless, as well as in the never-ending struggle to find ways of keeping tobacco in our pipes and food of any sort on the table. For reasons I only came to understand later when my friend's work at Bletchley Park became known to me, foreign-language newspapers, even those from countries with which we were at war – amongst many others *La Repubblica* from Italy, the *Völkischer Beobachter* from Germany and newspaper of the National Socialist party, and *Le Figaro* from Vichy France would arrive daily from Lisbon, flown in specially, I was told – and Holmes would dedicate himself every evening to a perusal of these.

The one illumination in the all-pervading gloom would come when Holmes placed his Stradivarius under his chin. His caseload in the 1890s meant that he had neglected his violin for most of the last half-century, but now it provided a welcome escape from these dark times – certainly for me and maybe even for him. Rather than extemporising unmelodiously with the instrument slung across his lap as had been his wont in our Baker Street days, he would play one favourite piece of mine after another, displaying a dash and skill that could not be surpassed. There was no rationing or short supply when Holmes's violin came out of its case.

He himself was dissatisfied with his performance and dedicated himself to practice as well as to display. Even when he broke a string, something very hard to replace in wartime Britain, he carried on his playing undaunted. "If I can make a fist of playing my music on three strings," he remarked, "how much better will I be able to play it when I eventually get a full complement back? Making a hard task even harder, means its accomplishment is facilitated once that additional difficulty has been overcome."

Holmes proved the truth of this remark in a way that was entirely unexpected to me.

After much fruitless writing to music-shops and suppliers of equipment, a night-time road accident in the village, an event all too common in blacked-out Britain despite the lack of cars on the road, brought down a telegraph pole, and my friend approached the engineer who had come to fix the line.

"It's more than my job's worth to help anyone these days," was the engineer's initial response between bites of a sandwich he was eating for his lunch when Holmes first spoke to him on the lane.

But then my friend identified himself and offered as a *quid pro quo* a pot of honey from the hives.

The engineer quipped, "To say that I helped restore the violin of the great Mr Sherlock Holmes will be a wonderful story to tell if they have any beer next time I am down at the pub."

"I had thought," said my friend when he told me about this afterwards, "that if the engineer had failed to be tempted by my honey, I might point out that the fresh egg I could see in the sandwich he was eating must have come from some other irregular trade of his – these days a fresh egg is a special event not to be sacrificed in a casually consumed lunchtime sandwich."

"I am sure everyone in a position to supply goods of any sort that are otherwise unobtainable is up to that sort of trick," I grunted, slightly sourly, as I had not set eyes on a fresh egg for several weeks.

"Maybe in my advanced years, good Watson," said Holmes, paying little heed to my comment, and less to my demeanour, "I am acquiring that skill of diplomacy which you have so often stated I lack. My use of what I might call a honey-trap, was just as efficient in getting what I wanted as the unwelcome insight into a man's personal habits I might otherwise have deployed. It is always better to have a threat available as well as a reward when trying to persuade someone to do something he might otherwise be reluctant to do."

It was the work of a moment for Holmes to fit the fine steel wire he had obtained in this barter from the telegraph engineer to his fiddle. His instrument now once more equipped with its full number of strings, the music rose from under his fingers with a still more beguiling poetry and fire, and so helped pass many a cold, dark, damp, and worrying evening.

Occasionally Holmes and I would ramble together through the flat countryside that surrounded us just as we had rambled through the streets of London half a century and more previously, and it was at two o'clock on the afternoon of Friday the 22nd of November 1940 that we turned into the lane in which our cottage stood from one such walk and were overtaken by a black car which stopped at our gate.

"I can only assume that it is a government vehicle," murmured Holmes thoughtfully, "so I can only assume that there is someone from the government who wants to see me."

In the England of 1940, petrol for private motoring was unobtainable, and so official cars of one sort or another were the only ones on the road. If a car stood outside our door, it really could only be because someone from the government wanted to see Holmes.

Again, I confess I considered Holmes's deduction something of a statement of the obvious, and I think Holmes read this thought on my face as he gave a slightly wan smile before adding, "Shortages of basic supplies render even the art of deduction both unchallenging and unrevealing at present, I fear."

As we got to the gate that marked the entry to our property, a uniformed chauffeur got out of the car.

"Mr Holmes and Dr Watson?" he asked, and we both nodded. "I have an urgent summons for the attendance of you two gentlemen at an office in Whitehall."

It was a two-hour drive from Fenny Stratford. Apart from the almost complete absence of cars on the road to which I have already alluded, in country areas the journey was much as it would have been in peace time. But, once we arrived at the north-western environs of London, we saw the transformation that the bombing war had wrought. Beige barrage balloons bobbed unsteadily above us and, as we passed the RAF airbase of Northolt, we saw the damage that raids targeted on it had inflicted – though the damage was to the houses that surrounded it rather than to the aerodrome itself.

And the scars of the air-war only became more apparent as we got into central London. Our car passed whole districts that had been reduced to yellow-grey swathes of brick rubble. There were red buses but many of them towed a trailer with producer gas behind them. And of course, just as we did ourselves, everyone carried a gas-mask.

The car drew up at the Foreign Office in King Charles Street, and we were shown upstairs to the office of the Under-Secretary of State for Foreign Affairs.

Richard Austen Butler, or Rab Butler as he was always known from the sound spelt by the initials of his name, was the deputy of this country's Foreign Secretary. He had a higher political profile than might be expected from someone with the title Under-Secretary, for he was the representative of the Foreign Office in the House of Commons, as the Foreign Secretary, Lord Halifax, as the title preceding his name suggests, sat in the House of Lords.

Butler, although only thirty-eight, looked weary with care. He proffered each of us a rather weak handshake and we sat down.

"In the last decade," he began, "I supported the attempts by the government of Neville Chamberlain to achieve a rapprochement with Germany. I was in favour of the Munich settlement for Czechoslovakia, and I was against giving the Poles any sort of a guarantee that we would intervene if they were invaded, particularly once the Poles had appropriated Czechoslovak territory after the Germans took over the rest of Czechoslovakia at the beginning of last year. And, even after the fall of France, our defeat in Norway, and the Germans' pact with the Soviets, I remain of the opinion that a solution to the present conflict in Europe can be achieved based on common-sense rather than bravado."

I think he was expecting a reaction from either Holmes or me, but I had nothing to say, and Holmes stayed silent. Butler rose and started pacing the room.

"With the defeat of our French allies, we have no means to prosecute this war to a successful conclusion. Although the superiority of our Navy renders the chances of a successful land invasion here negligible, we lack the manpower and the war materiel to land and maintain troops on the European mainland in sufficient numbers to drive the Germans out of France and the Low Countries, let alone to liberate Poland, which was the original *casus belli*, and out of the rest of eastern Europe. Attempts to continue the war in Europe will only sap this nation's ability to maintain dominion over its global Empire which is where its vital interests lie."

"I note, Under-Secretary, that you do not mention the possibility of other alliances."

"Our alliances to date have brought us nothing. We may even have been better off without an alliance with the Soviets as last autumn saw them preferring a pact with the Germans before they first struggled to subdue the Poles, who had already been invaded by the Germans from the west, and then the Finns, whom they outnumbered by ten to one."

Butler sighed heavily.

"What would we not give for an American intervention in this conflict? But their ambassador, Joseph Kennedy, has just published an article saying that we are finished as a democracy so no help can be sought from that quarter at present, as his opinion cannot be far from that of President Roosevelt. Indeed, when the President was re-elected at the beginning of the month, our telegraph of congratulation had to be sent twice before it was acknowledged. And the Americans have their own disagreements with the Japanese in the Pacific, and these affect them much more directly than a war in Europe. They are thus far more likely to engage themselves on their western sea-board and beyond than to concern themselves with events two-thousand miles to their east in Europe."

He paused before continuing.

"With our Empire and our Navy, it is this country's destiny to dominate the world, and leave Germany, with its military might, industrial strength, and central location, to dominate mainland Europe. Our only interest in Europe is to ensure that any conflicts there take place as far away from us as possible, so as to minimise their effect on us. Over the last eighty years, the main fault-line has been between France and Germany, as we have seen with the Franco-Prussian War and then the Great War, as they squabble over deposits of coal and iron-ore in Alsace-Lorraine. Now the British front line consists of the airfields of the south-east of England, which the Germans spent the last summer bombarding, and our harbours, in which the Germans continue to lay mines. And what am I, as Under-Secretary of State for Foreign Affairs, tasked with?" he concluded plaintively.

Again, neither Holmes nor I had any comment to make.

"I am the Foreign Secretary's deputy, a man fluent in both German and French, and I have spent significant amounts of time in both countries. But my responsibilities are confined to ensuring the welfare of our prisoners-of-war and arranging for the safe passage of diplomats. And I am only allowed even that meagre range of activities because I enjoy the protection of the Foreign Secretary, Lord Halifax, who concurs with me on what measures are necessary for the benefit of the nation but who may be relieved of his present role at any time, and whose endorsement of the present Prime Minister's bellicose posturing is for public consumption only. A different Foreign Secretary may take steps to circumscribe what I am allowed to do even more."

"Minister," said Holmes at length, "while I note your views, and while I appreciate the candour with which you express them, this does not explain why you have summoned Dr Watson and me to London."

"I mentioned that one of my responsibilities is the welfare of our prisoners-of-war. Healthy prisoners are normally held until the conflict has come to an end, while wounded or otherwise infirm prisoners are held until they are swapped. Thus, each side bears the direct cost of caring for its wounded and we can bring our wounded heroes back to where they can get the care of their loved ones. But our calamitous defeats in Norway and then in France mean that we have very few wounded Germans whom we can swap for our own prisoners, while at

Dunkirk alone forty thousand of our men were taken prisoner – a fact that is often overlooked in the excitement of the successful evacuation of three-hundred thousand men. We have, it is true, shot down some of their airmen but shooting down fighters and bombers does not deliver many prisoners to swap. It is victory in land-battles that do that, and we have no victories to show for nearly a year and half of war."

"So, what is our brief?"

"I want you, Dr Watson, to present to the Germans the bleakest assessment of our prisoners' condition, and you, Mr Holmes, to use the acumen for which you are renowned to maximise the ratio of prisoners they will then release in exchange for the German prisoners that we hold."

"But will our fellow countrymen not regard the return of large numbers of prisoners-of-war as showing a crack in this country's resolve to prosecute this war?"

"In a few months' time we will be in the third year of the war. As things look at present, we will have nothing to show for it other than military defeat, isolation that is far from splendid, shredded living standards, and poor prospects. The third year of any major undertaking – particularly a hazardous one such as this one – is generally when the willingness to continue starts to wane. So, I believe that, at some point next year, national resolve will waver, and that the return of prisoners in numbers will be welcomed as a harbinger of the return of more normal times. As such a return will have been accomplished when we have very few prisoners to swap with them, it will also demonstrate that the Germans are biddable, and consequently that acceptable arrangements can be reached for the government of Europe."

"Why have you chosen us for this task?"

"I am aware from Dr Watson's writings Mr Holmes, that, like me, you both know French and German – indeed your first *coup de maître* as a detective, Mr Holmes, was to identify that the letters RACHE on a wall of a crime-scene spelt the German word for vengeance where Inspector Lestrade thought that they were the first five letters of the name Rachel. Giving this mission to two notables such as yourselves, whom the Germans will consider trustworthy, will also assure them of the extreme seriousness with which we take the welfare of our prisoners, and our wish to ensure that our wounded get treatment in their own country. And, clearly, at the age you have both reached, employing you for this task will mean that we are not sacrificing men of fighting age to achieve these objectives."

"And how will we carry out this role from England?"

"You will not be in England. On the contrary, you will be given diplomatic status for you are needed abroad. An aircraft is leaving Bristol Whitchurch tomorrow night for Lisbon, and I want you to be on it. At Lisbon you will be met by Hans Frölicher, the Swiss Ambassador to Germany. You may place some trust in him although I would urge you to avoid doing so if you can. From Lisbon you will travel by train across the Iberian Peninsula, and thence through Vichy France to Geneva. In Geneva you will be attached to the Red Cross which has its headquarters there, but your stay there will be brief as Frölicher will accompany you to Berlin and facilitate meetings there with the German high-command."

It was news to me that it was possible for members of the general public to leave the country for Continental Europe at all, let alone go to Berlin, and I think Butler saw my look of puzzlement.

"The United Kingdom," he said, "still has vital interests to defend on Continental Europe which are mostly prosecuted on our behalf by the Swiss. We cannot go to Switzerland by a direct route so a flight to Lisbon and a long haul from there by train is the way the journey is normally made. The journey is, I confess, not without its perils, but there have as yet been no attempts by the Germans to bring down the KLM 'planes that fly across the western English Channel and the Bay of Biscay to Lisbon and, once in Portugal, our emissaries to Switzerland are treated by the Portuguese, Spanish, and Vichy French authorities as if they were a diplomatic bag so no attempt is made to interfere with their progress. That is how our own prisoners-of-war who escape capture and make it to Switzerland are eventually brought home."

I remained unconvinced by Butler's statement, but he continued.

"There is a similar 'plane from Dublin to Lisbon which doubtless carries the German ambassador there when he needs to consult face to face with Berlin. I cannot imagine there are many Irish businessmen needing a commercial flight to Lisbon just at the moment. Nor, I suppose, are there many Irish people heading to the Algarve on holiday. So, I assume it is largely used by the Germans for espionage matters. We have not tried to down that 'plane either. And that 'plane is a daily one whereas the flight from Whitchurch to Lisbon only goes three times a week. Although we are at war with Germany, you will appreciate that there are still matters where there is a mutual understanding of what is acceptable, and of what is not. Or, perhaps, to put it more precisely, where we both think we can prosecute the war more effectively by not aggressing against each other. And that rather parallels what we are seeking to achieve here."

The meeting concluded and we headed down the grandiose Foreign Office staircase for the street-door. We went to the reception desk to say we were ready to return to Fenny Stratford, when an official appeared as if from nowhere, and murmured, "I fear, gentlemen, the car that brought you here from Fenny Stratford has been requisitioned for another purpose. You will need to make your own way home although we will of course pay for your travel costs. I would suggest you walk along the Thames to Embankment Station and take the Northern Line to Euston from there."

Holmes was philosophical about the turn of events. "I fancy," said he turning to me, "that your chronicles of my activities only had us leave London from Euston Station at the time of *The Stockbroker's Clerk* when we went to Birmingham, so it is high time another of our adventures started from there."

It was by now after five o'clock on a late November evening, and we passed through the black-out curtains and out of the Foreign Office front-door. Depending on when this work is read, the scene that confronted us as we stood on the steps of the Foreign Office will either cause my reader to wonder why I draw attention to it as it will be entirely what is expected, or it will seem totally alien.

As we left the foreign office building, we extinguished the cigarettes we were both smoking in line with regulations on smoking in the black-out that had been in place since the outbreak of the war. Once outside, the buildings of London, so familiar in daylight, were in complete and utter darkness. This was no different from Fenny Stratford, but there I was unaccustomed to going out in the night hours whereas, having lived in London for most of the half century preceding the mid-1930s, I was back in surroundings where I was used to lighting at night.

But now, while I could hear both the footfalls and the voices of pedestrians as they hurried past, as well as the groan of trams, the hum of bus engines, and the hissing of trolley buses, standing on those steps, I could see nothing.

My reader may wonder whether we had pocket torches. Normally we would have done, but these had a long extension protruding from above the bulb preventing their beam being seen from the air and this meant they cast only the feeblest beam – enough to follow the pavement on which alternate kerb stones had been painted black and white to facilitate finding the way in the dimmest light – but not much more. And because this extension makes them awkward to carry, and because we had in any case thought we would have transport back to Fenny Stratford, it had not occurred to us to take these with us.

So it was, that Holmes and I followed the route that had been suggested to us along the north bank of the Thames.

For my part, I was reassured to hear the sound of the water lapping against the stone of the Embankment and the motors of watercraft on the river, but I still found my surroundings utterly alien. For his part, Holmes, with his intimate knowledge of all London's thoroughfares and his preternatural ability, assiduously cultivated by him to see in the dark what others could not – as he had demonstrated back in the case of *The Speckled Band* – was far more at ease than I was.

"How long would I survive now against my own pursuit?" his assured voice broke cheerily through the blackness, quoting directly his words from *The Bruce-Partington Plans*. "In fog, I commented in 1895, all it would take to get me was a bogus appointment for a pursuer to come to do what he had to do, and then disappear into thin air. I commented that it was fortunate that South America, continent of assassinations, has no fog. But now, in this country with its total blackness, an assassin would need know no more than my whereabouts to have me at his mercy."

Some pedestrians, I noted, as we walked the half mile along the riverside to Embankment Station, wore phosphorescent pins which glimmered eerily in the blackness to draw one's attention to their presence, but which provided no other illumination. The outdoor smoking ban meant that one could not even smell tobacco to alert one of the presence of other people, while the occasional public transport vehicle that passed us had blacked out windows, although flashes from the overhead cables of the trams and trolley-buses did very occasionally provide an intense but brief illumination. The only visible betrayal of a vehicle's presence was a sliver of light that was emitted through a slit in the hood cowling its lamp.

It was a relief to get to Embankment Underground Station where, sensibly, we were permitted to light up our cigarettes once we had finally got down to platform level although, as one would expect, as at all stations, smoking was banned in the entry hall.

I drew heavily on my cigarette as we waited for our train, eagerly sucking in its soothing smoke, and I noted Holmes doing the same. After six stops, we got to Euston, and onto our train to Bletchley. I knew better than to discuss our commission with Holmes in a public place. Thus, once on our heavily blinded train, my cigarettes having run out, I confined my activities to making the meagre amount of tobacco I had left in my pouch last the length of our journey in my pipe. Holmes too confined himself to making his remaining supply of tobacco last as long as possible, and we exchanged not a word until we reached Bletchley.

The next morning Holmes and I sat over a breakfast of greyish bread covered with a few streaks of margarine accompanied by some equally greyish tea. My friend was in an excellent mood. "It is good to be engaged in something that will tax my mind particularly at this time of year which is the quietest one for the apiarist."

"How do you view our brief?" I asked.

"It is not my business to comment on the Under-Secretary's views on policy, but I feel that we are equipped as well as anyone else in the country would be to secure a favourable bargain with the Germans on this matter. I have a reputation that will ensure we are taken seriously, and you have a way with words which will place the best construction on anything we seek to negotiate."

More Wartime Journeying

Any sort of wartime journey is not to be undertaken lightly.

Fenny Stratford to Whitchurch by train would have required a return to London and a journey to Bristol via Paddington. We were fortunate that a car was again placed at our disposal, and we traversed the one hundred and twenty miles in under four hours.

It was just getting dark as we reached Whitchurch, where waiting on the grass was a black painted 'plane. A Douglas Commercial 3, I was told. But it was one o'clock in the morning by the time we were allowed to walk across the runway turf and, with fourteen other intrepid passengers, board the craft. Our numbers filled the cabin and parachutes were handed out.

We bumped down the runway and took off. The pilot came over the intercom.

"Most of you will be regular travellers on this flight but, for those of you who are new to it, our flight time to Lisbon will be five hours assuming the enemy takes no interest in us. I cannot disclose to you our precise route, but a look at a map will show you that we need to fly over seas whose shorelines are held by the enemy or by non-belligerent but hostile powers. We will therefore be well out to sea on our journey – as far as possible out of reach of their fighters – and will be flying low to evade enemy radar."

I had never been on a commercial aircraft before – I had seen pictures before the outbreak of the war which had made flying look glamorous, but a seat in a cramped, blacked-out cabin in the dead of night was anything but that. Even smoking was prohibited in the early part of the flight. I tried to sleep but the roar from the engine made this impossible. After about an hour I gently pulled back the black-out curtain and looked out at the scene. At first I thought that here too was only blackness, but my eyes slowly got accustomed to the surroundings which received illumination from a quarter moon that emerged now and then from behind louring cloud cover. Occasionally I could look down onto the sea which, as the captain had warned, was alarmingly close to us. But for the deafening roar of the engine, I suspect I could have heard the waves, and it was a huge relief when, after what seemed an eternity, the captain's voice came over the intercom that we were about to land at Lisbon Airport.

It was just light, and we came to a halt two - hundred yards from the airport building. As we walked across the runway grass towards it, it was an unwonted sight that greeted our eyes. German and British 'planes – respectively distinguished by their markings of a black cross or a red, white, and blue roundel – stood parked next to each other, although I noted that each 'plane was guarded by a Portuguese soldier.

"Truly Lisbon airport is the hub of today's espionage," murmured Holmes. "Missions start, end, and have their intermissions here. There cannot be many places in Europe like it."

As Butler had arranged, Hans Frölicher, the Swiss ambassador to Berlin, was waiting for us at the airport building. He was to play a major role in the events that followed, and we had two days in close quarters with him as we traversed Portugal, Spain, and Vichy France to get to Geneva.

This journey was marred by endless checks of identity papers particularly as we crossed borders but took no longer than it would have done in peace-time as British bombers had not by this stage of the war targeted southern French railways.

Our first evening in Switzerland destroyed any notion I might have had that neutrality bestowed plenty on the Swiss. I had not been to Switzerland since my time at Lausanne investigating the disappearance of Lady Frances Carfax. Then, the hotels were luxurious, and Switzerland a delightful place. Now Geneva and, I suspect, all Swiss cities, were quite hollowed out by the war. The city streets were at least lit at night, and, particularly after the darkness of London, it was disconcerting to see lights winking, perhaps a little uncertainly, in the night, although the glow they cast was feeble at best.

"We do not have a black-out here," explained Frölicher, "but we have greatly reduced lighting as an austerity measure. Switzerland imports all the fuel it uses and is now completely surrounded by Axis states which use coal and oil supplies as leverage against us."

Early December 1940 was bitterly cold, and thick frost lined the insides of our windows at our hotel.

"Most flats have one designated warm room in which a fire is made up using foraged wood and pinecones as coal is so short, and leave the rest of the flat unheated," said Frölicher. "You can imagine how cold that leaves them in weather like this, and our winter will last until at least the end of March."

And we discovered at dinner what happens to potatoes when their storage place freezes. They turn black and their waxy consistency makes them almost inedible. But you will eat them when there is nothing else. We were in what would have been in more normal times, an international hotel. And there was nothing else available to eat for supper that night.

At breakfast the next morning, the bread - and there was not much else on offer - was completely dry.

"We aren't allowed to give you bread on the day it is made," said our waiter, as I queried why he had nothing better. "It means you eat less of it. And by and large, there is in any case nothing else to give you. My wife has given me some of the beechnuts she foraged at the cemetery when they fell from the trees last month."

"Beechnuts? What do they taste like?" I asked in some wonder.

"I'll swap you one for a slice of the bread you have taken such exception to," said he. "Once you've tasted a beechnut, you won't want another if you can get hold of bread - even bread that's a day old."

This opinion I was able to confirm by the bitter taste in my mouth caused by the beechnut's ingestion which several glasses of water – and even this was hard to get hold of as many pipes were frozen solid - were unable to erase.

Looking at the thin, haggard people on the street as we walked to Geneva's main station, you wondered what they were eating, and I put this to Frölicher.

"I am based in Berlin and as a diplomat I have the means to make my diet a little more varied than that of the average Swiss. Before the war, half of our food was imported, and while we can still import some, we simply have to eat less, and produce more for ourselves. But the situation in Germany is not that much easier because you British blockade the German ports, just as you did in the previous war. Then the Germans nearly starved. So far they have been able to maintain food supplies, but it is not clear how long they will be able to do it, or how they will solve their problem of food supply other than through further conquests. British policy makes further attempts by the Germans to invade those neighbours of theirs that they have not yet attacked only more likely."

Our journey to Berlin was scheduled to take us from Geneva to Zurich and then up through Constance, Munich, and Leipzig. "But your country's bombing raids may well mean we have to make a detour or two," said Herr Frölicher, a slight note of reproach in his voice.

As it was, the journey was uneventful, even though twenty-three hours is a long time in a train.

"Only seven hours more than it would take in peacetime," sighed Frölicher, as we got into the outskirts of the city. "The main line from the south into Berlin was struck by one of your landmines ten days ago, so we have been detoured through various stretches of lines to the south-east of the city used by suburban services. The Berliners call it the S-Bahn. They will tell you the S stands for Schnell or 'fast' but the trains," Frölicher broke off to point out of the window as an electric powered S-Bahn train – coloured the red of London buses and the dun of London brick, the random thought struck me – trundled past, "are only fast compared to any alternative means of conveyance."

I looked out of the window.

"Those look like allotments with houses," I commented, looking at frost covered patches of ground with various structures like pergolas and cloches for the small-scale cultivation of fruit and vegetables, but with the addition of what looked like small and simple dwelling places built at the side.

"Ah yes. This is what the Germans call a Schrebergarten. That was the idea of a Doctor Schreber of Leipzig who thought that if people have a plot of land to cultivate, that would be good for their mental well-being as well as giving them a chance to grow food. Goodness knows, people need enough of both at present. Tenants of these allotments are allowed to build simple houses on the plot too, so these allotments are often called Gartenkolonien or garden-colonies. Some people choose to live in those houses at least in summer but, with your air-raids, they are an attractive place to live outside the centre of the city. Although the British air raids are so inaccurate, one's location in the city hardly makes any difference to one's personal safety and I suspect one is as likely to be struck by a British bomb here as in the city centre."

We had established in Geneva that the neediest British prisoners-of-war were housed in Lichterfelde, to the south of Berlin, and we went straight there on arrival in Berlin, where we were introduced to the commanding officer of the British forces, Brigadier le Couillard, who had been briefed on the reason for our appointment.

"Mine's a Channel Islands name originally," he said, "but I'd be as English as roast beef – if there were any available. The hospital here specialises in burns and there's one close at hand where our chaps go if they're getting a bit queer in the attic. Happens quite easily if you're cooped up in here. I got captured in France, so I've been here for six months, and God knows when I'll get back to Blighty."

"Our brief is to identify the sickest and neediest," I said, "to organise a prisoner-of-war swap with the Germans"

"Well, I've organised a hundred candidates for you – burns, wounds, and head-cases. Up to you to rank them, I suppose."

"I should like to see them."

We were soon in the burns unit.

"Most of these chaps are tank crew. Some air-crew," said le Couillard. "Battle of France mainly. A few from the bombing raids on Berlin. Their tanks brew up. Or air-crew try to land their craft and get burnt on the way down or when they try to eject from their 'planes."

The first one we saw was called Raglan. He had come down over the Channel, during what is now called the Battle of Britain, although it had not acquired that name at the time.

Raglan did not have, I thought, long left. The parts of his skin not covered by bandages had a glassy sheen, and he looked disinterested by his surroundings.

"I am not sure he would survive what would be a hazardous journey back to England," I commented bleakly to le Couillard.

I made the same comment about a number of other victims and in the end le Couillard grunted, "Well you'd better see one of our head-cases. Much harder to persuade the Germans that they really need to be taken home. The Germans make out that they're trying it on to get out, and will recover miraculously once back on our side, and will then re-join the ranks. But there's no shortage of them."

"My real enemy is the French," said the first one, Westcott. "They let the Germans through to attack us."

"They really didn't," interjected le Couillard. "They held our line outside Dunkirk and enabled our evacuation to take place behind it."

"Whatever they did, they didn't help me or else I wouldn't be here. And you've got a French name," said Westcott accusingly, looking at the brigadier.

"Do I sound in any way French?" le Couillard asked Westcott mildly.

"And Mr Holmes here was constantly helping the French rather than the British?"

I suspect that le Couillard had heard Westcott's opinions about the French before, but this remark about my friend excited the brigadier's curiosity, and he asked Westcott to expand.

"In *The Golden Pince-Nez*, Mr Holmes is referred to as having arrested the Boulevard assassin for which he won the Order of the Legion of Honour as well as receiving a personal letter from the French President. But in *The Three Garridebs*, he turns down a knighthood. He would only have behaved like that if he had been in the pay of the French."

Holmes had never previously had to defend his patriotism. He had just opened his mouth to do so when Westcott added.

"And it would be hard to imagine a more French name than Lestrade, and you helped him far more than you helped any other detective."

"I have served my country in every way I have been able to. Just as I am doing now," said Holmes, at an apparent loss for an answer for the first time in our long friendship.

The next soldier we saw was called Madson.

"I know their secret," he said.

He looked at le Couillard. "And I've told you all this before. How could an army the same size as the French and us combined advance eight hundred miles ahead of its border and take only a tenth of the casualties? We had twice the number of heavy guns and twice the number of tanks. There should only have been one winner when they attacked."

"There doesn't seem much point in discussing that now," mumbled le Couillard.

"It's down to this," said Madson, reaching into his pocket to pull out a grey tube. "I shot a German when I was defending the perimeter of Dunkirk. I went through his pockets and found this."

"Not your magic potions again, Madson," groaned le Couillard. "I've heard that one so often before."

"It's called Pervitin, and with it you can march faster, further, and longer. I'm sure that was how they were able to beat us," Madson continued, quite unperturbed by his superior's lack of interest in his thesis.

"They punched a hole in the French lines with massed tanks and bottled us up at the coast. It was better tactics, not some elixir giving them superhuman powers," replied le Couillard wearily.

I felt that Westcott and Madson both comfortably satisfied the twin criteria of being peculiar enough to persuade the Germans that they would not stage a recovery once back in Britain and of being robust enough to survive the journey.

We spent the rest of the day seeing soldiers of all sorts and I was relieved when the evening finally came.

Holmes and I were lodged at the Adlon Hotel in Berlin's famous boulevard, Unter den Linden or Under the Linden Tees. It is next door to the building that had housed the British Embassy in happier times. As I write these words, Unter den Linden is called the Stalinallee or Stalin Avenue, and the Adlon Hotel lies in ruins as, having survived the capture of Berlin, it was burnt to the ground by a drunk Russian soldier who set fire to the wine cellar.

The Adlon's concierge, Obermann, had been briefed about our stay. "I will make the best arrangements I can for you in these unpromising circumstances," he assured us. "I have enough connections that I can normally get hold of most things. I have read your works, Dr Watson," he said, addressing me, "and through my sources I have been able to get you a pack of your favourite Bradleys of Oxford Street cigarettes. I have made sure they are in your room." There was no equivalent gift for Holmes – I had been careful never to disclose his favourite tobacco in my accounts of our adventures - but I could see my friend was impressed by Obermann's resourcefulness.

The hotel was running as normal even in wartime, although uniforms were much in evidence amongst the guests in the imposing reception rooms on the ground floor. In one was gathered a party of Luftwaffe officers who were singing what sounded from its jaunty tune like a song to accompany a mountain walk. One line of the text ran, I recall, "Wir steigen zum Tor der Sonne empor" or "We climb up to the gate of the sun". It was not until the last line of the chorus was sung, fortissimo – "'Ran an den Feind, 'ran an den Feind, Bomben auf Eng-el-land" or "Up at the enemy, up at the enemy, Drop bombs on Eng-el-land" that the song's true import was clear to me.

Two doors down, was another reception room – deserted this time. I noticed there was a cabinet-gramophone in this one.

"Stille Nacht" or "Silent night" was issuing slightly cloyingly from it.

It sounded wildly incongruous following what was being sung with such gusto only a few steps away.

A Meeting with Joseph Goebbels

"You must call him Herr Dr Goebbels or Herr Reichsleiter," hissed the Swiss diplomat to us about the man we were about to meet. "He has a higher degree in literature, has published several books, is Imperial Minister for Propaganda and the Enlightenment of the People, and has the position in the government of leader of the Reich."

"Isn't Hitler the leader and Himmler the Reichsführer," I asked slightly puzzled as to how to distinguish all the leadership titles.

"This is a country where everyone has the title of a leader. Even though the person who makes all the decisions is Hitler."

"Where everybody is somebody, nobody is anybody," I quipped.

"I would simply say," responded Frölicher, slightly stiffly, as we crossed the threshold into Goebbels's imposing office in the Propaganda Ministry on the Wilhelmsplatz, "you will make your job here far more difficult if you do not call people by their right title, and Herr Reichsleiter is the term you should use. Herr Doktor Goebbels is also the Gauleiter or district leader of Berlin."

Goebbels rose and as we entered and walked falteringly towards us. I recalled that one of his feet was turned in, and this badly affected his gait.

"So, Herr Holmes, you have come to see your prisoners-of-war. Well, we have certainly captured plenty of them during our victories over the British in the last year on the Western front, Norway, and elsewhere. And who knows where we will be able to beat you next? To our north is Sweden with its iron ore, to our south is the Mediterranean where we may make our conquests render passage of your ships through the Suez Canal and the Straits of Gibraltar rather more hazardous than it is at present, and your own British islands lie to our west - if we feel your conquest is of strategic value. At our backs, we have our allies, the Soviets, from whom we get regular and plentiful supplies of cheap oil and animal feed as well as chrome, asbestos, and phosphates. I recall your attempts to secure the Soviets as allies of your own – one of British diplomacy's less glorious moments. But, dear Mr Holmes, we have beaten you on the battlefield and have beaten you at the negotiating tables. Our war is won. It is really now just a question of how it can be ended."

"I am not here, Herr Reichsleiter, to discuss the fortunes of war. I am here on a humanitarian mission on behalf of our prisoners-of-war. Dr Watson and I have visited several of the prisoner-of-war camps and we would like to reach an agreement with you on the repatriation of the sick and wounded ones. It would be of great comfort to them and to their families."

"I am sure the same would be true of our brave warriors in your hands. Except you hardly have any. I am not even sure why I am granting you an audience. We Germans want peace with Britain and her Empire, on terms which will allow a free Belgium, Netherlands, Luxembourg, Norway, and Denmark, and will also leave both France and Great Britain at liberty to pursue their imperial dreams wherever in the world you wish. All we want is a free hand in Eastern Europe, which is a place where the British and French have never had any significant interests."

Goebbels paused.

"Our country has been on a long journey, Mr Holmes. We used to have elections here in Germany, but my party was banned after the failed coup of

1923. Then we were allowed to reform, and in 1928 we stood for election, and got less than 3% of the vote. But there were still people who chose to be members of the National Socialist Party. They were heroes! They were routinely denounced in the press as inadequates or thugs or worse. Many faced criminal accusations on trumped up charges. But they were all good people."

Holmes was, I think, braced for a long diatribe, and reached for his pipe.

"I appreciate Mr Holmes that you are our visitor here," interrupted Goebbels, "but our Führer never lets tobacco smoke enter his body and our soldiers are not allowed to smoke when on duty. We are a very modern society. I would accordingly ask you not to light up here as smoking is banned in all our ministries."

In the end Holmes resorted to putting his pipe without tobacco to his lips and Goebbels continued.

"We made our stand on a battlefield that was not of our choosing. But if democracy chooses to give us the weapons to win power, then that is its problem. Any way of bringing about the revolution was fine by us, and within five years we were the biggest party. We didn't only get votes from the dispossessed. We got them from across society. Million people flocked to join our party. Then we struck a deal with President Hindenburg so that we could take power, and millions more flocked to join us. And, once we got power, we got the police records of our members wiped so that we could make a clean start ....."

At that moment, a brown-uniformed official burst into the meeting room. Goebbels looked annoyed at this interruption to his harangue, but the official whispered something into Goebbels's ear at which a look of utter horror came over the Reichsleiter's face. "You will excuse me gentlemen," he said, his voice suddenly quite shorn of its previous self-confidence. "A matter of the extreme importance has arisen, and I must postpone this meeting for another time."

We rose to do so and were just heading for the door, when Goebbels said, "But of course!"

He called us back.

"Mr Holmes," he said, "it is not something to be celebrated, but a criminal matter has arisen on which we could perhaps use your support."

Even in these surroundings as alien as any that could be imagined, Holmes's interest in criminal matters was undimmed. A light came into his eyes, and he reached into his pocket for his tobacco pouch and matches.

"Then, pray consult," murmured he, putting the few wisps of tobacco he had been able to extract from the base of his pouch into the bowl of his pipe, applying a match, and getting it to light only after an effort.

"Mr Holmes, we are engaged in a war that is more radical and more total than anyone could ever conceive. We occupy hostile territory that is three times the size of our own, over much of which we never planned to have hegemony, and all of which we have come into in the last two years. It is perhaps not surprising that these developments have had some unexpected consequences."

"Unexpected consequences are perhaps to be expected if one seeks to wage war more totally than has ever previously been conceived," replied Holmes drily.

"Your own country has declared a policy of unrestricted warfare," retorted Goebbels, "so I am not aware that what we are doing is all that different from what you are. Just as acquiring colonies covering large areas of the earth's surface is something that Britain has shown the world how to do. What we are doing is no more than getting what is our entitlement as a great nation delayed in its gestation."

I think that Goebbels expected a riposte to this, but Holmes merely continued to puff at his nearly empty pipe, and Goebbels continued.

"Berlin is now a city full of foreigners and low-lifes. Our party has made every effort to eliminate the scourge of Jews and Gypsies from our midst, but our military victories have meant that our manpower is away fighting and has had to be replaced by labour from two sources – women, whose place should be in the home, and manpower, from subject races whom we would not normally have countenanced accommodating in our midst."

In the company of Holmes, I had heard petitions from people of every background and on every subject, but this was couched in terms wildly different from any I had heard previously. I glanced across at Holmes to see how he was reacting to Goebbels's words, but he confined himself to saying.

"It is certainly true that we live in a time of unprecedented turbulence."

"Over the last three months, there have been three incidents involving women travelling at night on our S-Bahn, the commuter trains that reach from Central Berlin to the outskirts. By a matter of great good fortune, in the first two attacks, the women survived, although they had fallen from the train while it was moving at full speed between stations. Late last night or early this morning, there was another incident. I have no more details at this time than that this third incident also involved a woman, and that it was fatal. The victim's body has already been taken to the morgue but the nearest station to the scene of the crime is Karlshorst on a track to the south-east of the centre. It is a fortunate coincidence indeed that you have come to me as a petitioner and a task has arisen worthy of the greatest detective the world has known. I want you to investigate whether these incidents are connected and, if they are, who is behind them."

"Herr Doktor, this is a most unexpected turn of events. You will appreciate that I will need to obtain instructions from London on how to respond to your petition. A successful investigation of this crime, if a crime it be, will make it easier for Germany to conduct its war-effort, and that is something that may not be countenanced even if it results in the return of more of our prisoners."

"I can think of nothing else the British can offer me at this time. You have no prisoners to exchange, the area bombing raids which you have started are puny compared to what we can do because we have a larger bomber force, and our bombers can fly from northern France to London, which is a much shorter distance than from southern England to Berlin. And there is nowhere where you can mount forces to confront us on land in significant number."

Holmes asked for permission to consult with Frölicher and me, and this was granted.

"It pains me to say so," whispered Holmes in a little anteroom outside Goebbels's office, "but we really do have very little else to offer the Germans. This may be the only way to persuade him to release some prisoners."

"But Holmes," I objected, "this sequence of attacks might even be a plot by the British Secret

Services to disrupt Germany's war-effort. You don't want to conduct an investigation that results in the capture and hanging of a British spy."

There was silence as Holmes considered this point.

"I have no choice but to seek London's permission to investigate this matter," he said at length.

"You must assume that any connection from Switzerland to London will be compromised unless it is sent from outside Switzerland," said Frölicher. "I would suggest I go to Madrid and see the British ambassador there."

"But it will take three days for you to get to Madrid and wait for an answer, and then three days to get back." There was a pause. "Why do you not ask that the last item on the six o'clock news from the BBC on this Sunday, the 8th of December, be about

Switzerland? I will take such a report as a signal that we have the go-ahead to progress."

"How will you hear the BBC news here?"

"There is a wireless in our room, and I can tune it to London."

"That is a Volksempfänger or people's receiver – the wireless distributed by the National Socialists. It blocks foreign radio transmissions so you will not be able to pick up a BBC broadcast." Frölicher thought for a second and then reached into his brief-case. "Here, you may borrow the radio that I use. I will be able to pick a new one up when I pass through Switzerland on the way to Madrid. That is one of the advantages of being a diplomat."

"I will tell Goebbels that I will start on those aspects of the case where early investigation is paramount – examination of the crime scene and so on. I will not brief his officers, although I will ask them questions which may, I regret, give them an indication of my direction of thoughts before I get permission from London to prosecute this matter."

We returned to Goebbels's office. I was expecting Holmes to take the lead, but Frölicher jumped in before Holmes could speak.

"On the rail sidings in Romanshorn, at the border between our countries, are two train-loads of coal that have been held up. If you arrange for them to be released, I will make sure that a message is passed to London asking for permission for Mr Holmes to investigate your case."

"You have a nerve," retorted Goebbels. "You think you have one over me, so you want me to release coal. It might just be better if we sent two-hundred thousand of our soldiers across your border."

"We Swiss have one-hundred thousand trained men under arms. If you do what you say, our one-hundred thousand soldiers will simply be commanded each to shoot two bullets rather than the one that would be sufficient to defeat your invasion if the numbers were evenly matched."

For the first time I saw Goebbels blink.

He picked up the receiver of his phone and put a call through to ask for the release of the consignment. Holmes then outlined how he would start the investigation to which Goebbels assented.

"And I will need fifty of our severely wounded men released for repatriation as a gesture of good faith before I assent to the suggestion being put to London. While we wait for a response, Watson and I will talk to your investigators to find out about the crimes, but we will not brief them on our findings," said Holmes, following Frölicher's lead.

Goebbels assented to this too – in retrospect, Holmes might have asked for more prisoners to be released – and a few minutes later we were going down the steps of Goebbels's ministry on the way to this most unexpected of cases.

Karlshorst

It was much the easiest to get the train for the forty-five minute-journey from the Wilhelmsplatz to Karlshorst. We were accompanied by a man who was introduced to us as the Reichskriminaldirektor, or the Director of the Reich's criminal police force, Arthur Nebe. He was a tall, fair man with sharp blue eyes, dressed in a slate-grey, and distinctly threatening-looking uniform.

We sat on the S-Bahn train. There were blinds on the windows which made the interior dim even above ground, which was where we were for most of our journey, and in daylight. There had been the same precautions in London, but we had only seen the underground train in a tunnel, so I had not really noticed them. In the S-Bahn's interior I noted that half the light bulbs had been removed and the half that was left were low wattage so that they cast only a feeble glow.

Nebe noticed me look up at the ceiling.

"I am sure your blackout precautions in London are no different. This is second class. There is no first class on the S-Bahn. Third class is just as dark and much more crowded because it is half the price of second."

The detective who had been assigned to the investigation was called Wilhelm Lüdtke – an alert - looking man in his late fifties with thick but greying hair, brown eyes, and glasses. With his mobile features, he looked rather like an older version of Stanley Hopkins. He wore plain clothes.

From Karlshorst Station, we walked along the track to where the body lay.

"What was the name of the victim?" asked Holmes.

"Nothing was taken from the body, so we have her identity card," replied Lüdtke. "She was a nurse called Elfreede Franke and twenty-six years old. She was still in her nurse's uniform."

"And was her clothing disturbed in any way?"

"There was no sign of that. She had fallen from the train."

"Then it would appear that there was neither a robbery nor a sexual act. How sure are we that her precipitation from the train was the result of an attack?"

Nebe had listened to Holmes's questions with mounting impatience.

"We don't know anything. On the 20th of September of this year a factory worker, Miss Gerda Kargoll, complained that she had been attacked by a uniformed man on this stretch of line. She said she had been strangled and thrown from the train. She certainly left the train when it was moving at full speed, but she landed on a pile of sand, and so survived. She admitted that she had been drinking, had fallen asleep several times on the train, and had exceeded the journey that her ticket permitted her, so her complaints were not taken too seriously."

"You mean someone claimed to have been attacked and thrown from a moving train, yet you did not take the accusation too seriously?" I asked Lüdtke, slightly incredulous.

Lüdtke shrugged.

"I only have limited resources and the lady's story had the flaws my colleague has enumerated. We will probably need to speak to her again now. The second event was Elizabeth Bendorf in early November. With her there was no doubt that she sustained a horrific assault and that she was thrown from the train because, by some miracle, she survived the fall even though she did not have the good fortune to hit a mound of sand."

"On this stretch of line?"

"Yes."

Holmes remained silent and Lüdtke continued.

"Frau Bendorf's testimony had none of the defects from the first case, so we took investigating her claim very seriously. But we found nothing. Now we have this Elfreede Franke. We don't even know whether she was assaulted. She may have committed suicide."

"When was she found?"

"At half past four this morning by a member of station staff taking a shortcut along the tracks to get to his early morning shift."

"So, to summarise, gentlemen," interjected Holmes, "there have been three instances of women being found fallen or precipitated on the same stretch of railway tracks in the last three months. One claimed to have been strangled, one had undoubtedly been the subject of a vicious assault, and one cannot speak for herself as she is dead. Are there any other cases you would wish to draw to my attention?"

Lüdtke had opened his mouth to answer when a junior policeman – I could tell by the lack of decorations on his uniform – dashed up.

"We have found another body," he panted out.

"Where?" exclaimed Lüdtke and Nebe.

"In bushes outside Karlshorst Station."

"We will have to go back there," said Lüdtke, "unless there is anything else here you wish to see Mr Holmes?"

My friend shook his head briefly and Lüdtke turned to addressing his junior colleague.

"How was she found?" he asked.

"A man was out walking his dog and the animal became very restive when he passed the bush."

We were soon back at Karlshorst Station and went through the barriers onto the quiet street outside.

Although the cases I have seen fit to set before the public often feature a horribly mangled body, my focus was always on Holmes's skill as a reasoner, so I never made anything of it. I am however bound to say that I never saw a more savaged body than that of this next victim. She had not been robbed and the identity card in her handbag revealed her to be nineteen and called Irmgard Freese. But her skull was all crushed in – her tightly bound blonde plats were thickly clotted with blood – and the state of her clothing left no doubt as to the motive for the crime.

At Lüdtke's invitation, I examined the body.

"Initially struck from behind with a blunt object. The blow would have rendered her incapable of running away and the assailant then attacked from the front. The skull is quite crushed in. It was a frenzied attack. There are at least six major blows here, and any of them would have reduced the victim to unconsciousness, but the assailant continued. She must have been dead, or close to death, when her attacker added rape to his assault."

Nebe lit a cigarette.

"Two deaths in one night, one resulting in precipitation from a train, the other with a body found walking distance from a station. One confirmed assault resulting in ejection from a moving train. One person falling from a train and claiming they were assaulted. I think we must now attach more credence to that claim. And all against good German women going about their business. We have enemies within as well as enemies massed at our borders."

He paused and drew deeply on his cigarette.

"And yet there are as many differences in the cases as there are similarities. A strangulation, three assaults with a blunt object, a sexual motive present in only one case out of four, and no motive at all for the other three cases. It is not surprising when our country is full of degenerates. Two deaths." he added for emphasis. "A double event." A pause and he looked at Holmes. "Wasn't there a double event when Jack the Ripper was stalking London?"

"That was over fifty years ago."

"But in darkness."

"That is so. But the victims then were what was described in the parlance of the day as unfortunates. That description does not apply to any of the victims here."

"I always thought it was some conspiracy amongst the British aristocracy. And I would be astonished if you were not involved with the case Mr Holmes. Whether to investigate it. Or to cover it up."

"The Ripper case is not relevant here."

"Mr Holmes, we fight this war to make this country fit for true Germans to live in. And two key parts of that are our nation's capital, where the power is centred, and the railway system, which we use to move troops to defend our frontiers. And both depend on foreign labour. There are four hundred thousand foreign forced labourers in Berlin alone – that is more than ten per cent of the city's population and a fifth of the working population. The railways depend on them. And there is a camp at Wuhlheide – that's less than five kilometres from here – where the most criminal of them are quartered. I would be astonished if the criminal did not come from there."

"And are they allowed to roam freely at night?" asked Holmes mildly.

"Not officially, no. But we have got too soft. I am sure one of them got out and did this."

"And had managed to get hold of a uniform as worn by the attacker of Miss Kargoll?"

"We have a plague of people breaking into houses following bombing raids, even though such plundering is rightly punishable by death. Getting hold of a uniform – any old uniform for a darkened train in the black-out would do – is easy."

"And get back into their camp so that they can get out again and commit another crime?"

Nebe flushed angrily at Holmes questions.

He flung his cigarette down.

"Are your cases solved by not taking the facts seriously?"

"My cases are solved by establishing what the facts are."

"We know who our enemies are," growled Nebe eventually, as he ground its stub viciously into the dirt.

"So, you know that the perpetrator of this crime and, hence your enemy, is either a member of the British aristocracy or a foreign worker? Let us stick to what we really know. It is possible that there is more than one assailant at work here, but these four cases all occurred within walking distance of this train-line, three of them actually on the line, and two of them in one night. We must interview the other two victims you have mentioned."

"You seem, if I may say so, Mr Holmes, far too interested in finding the killer rather than in sending a warning to would-be imitators. How about one morning having ten forced labourers outside the camp at Wuhlheide dangling on the end of ropes with signs hung round their necks saying, 'I attacked German women'? That would have the required effect, whether we know who committed the actual crime or not."

"So, you think that a man who is capable of the vile acts we see here, will be dissuaded from perpetrating more by the sight of men hanging from a gallows?"

Silence from Nebe.

"We have gone soft, soft, I say," his voice grated out at last. "We have had far too many easy victories in the last few years, and we let others come in and do our work for us. These people only respect us if we act without mercy and aren't fussy as to whether we get the right people."

"And there have been no other attacks on women away from the trains in this area?"

Nebe and Lüdtke exchanged glances.

"Berlin is awash with crime. The darkness makes it easy," said Nebe at last.

"I asked whether there have been attacks on women."

More glances.

"On the edge of Berlin, there is a large stretch of land given over to allotments called the Gartenkolonie. Since the beginning of the year, there have been assaults on women there, as well as one violent death."

"And that is in this same south-eastern part of Berlin?"

"Yes."

"Did the criminal at the allotments act in the same way as the criminal on the train."

"Women were assaulted in the darkness and left for dead. We know no more about the allotment killer than we do about the train killer. But in the Gartenkolonie, the killer struck inside the house of the victim without any sign of forced entry, so he must have been known to her. The two women who were attacked on the train and who survived to say what happened were adamant that they did not know their attacker. We do not know if it is one person or several people behind this, or if one person is responsible for everything."

We were coming to the end of long day but there was still time to conduct interviews with the two women who had survived their assaults. Frau Kargoll, a slightly dishevelled figure, confirmed that she had been drinking on the night that she was attacked.

"It is so hard when my fiancé is on service. A glass of beer, maybe two. It is a comfort. The man who attacked me," she said, "saw me start when I realised I had missed my stop. He told me I could sit with him in second-class. Very polite he was. And then he suddenly gripped me by the throat."

She started to sob at the memory.

"I fought and I fought. And then I realised he was forcing me towards the door of the train. He pulled the handle of the door. He had a dark uniform on, but uniforms don't tell you much these days. Everyone is in one now."

"Can you remember anything about him?"

"I think he was about twenty-five and very strong."

She started to sob again and nothing else of any merit could be obtained from her.

Elizabeth Bendorf gave a far more collected impression. A tall thirty-year old, she gave the feeling of being able to handle most things.

"I am a railway employee," she said. "On the night of the 4th of November, I got onto a train at Hirschgarten Station at the end of my shift"

"Did you sit in the second or third-class compartment?"

"A man in a uniform signalled with his hand that I could sit in second-class. I was tired after a long shift selling tickets, and that meant I had the compartment to myself. In retrospect I should have been more suspicious."

"And what happened?"

"The man in the railway company uniform sat opposite me and started to make small talk."

"What did he discuss?"

"The usual topics. The weather, rations, his opinion of our leaders," she gave a slightly nervous glance at the uniformed Nebe. "And then, without warning, he reached into the sleeve of his jacket…

"Which sleeve?"

"He struck me here," she pointed to the left side of her skull, "so it was with the right hand. So, he would have taken his weapon from his left sleeve."

"Can you describe him?"

"In the dim light it was hard to make out anything, but he was about forty years old, of average build, and wearing a uniform."

"What uniform?"

"There are so many uniforms. I assumed it was one associated with the railway because he acted as though he had authority on the railway, but I did not look at the detail of it."

"But you work on the railways."

"There are thousands of people working on the railway. Germans and foreigners. And they all wear uniforms. And there are different uniforms for ticket-sellers, ticket-collectors, drivers, guards, track-layers, signalmen, cleaners, and train maintenance people. And in wartime, everyone is in uniform. And the light was dim. So, I cannot give a firm undertaking that it was a railway worker who attacked me."

Nocturnal Disturbances

We retired to our hotel.

The interior was not as chilly as our hotel in Geneva, if only because the weather in Berlin was noticeably warmer than in the Swiss city. Nevertheless, our rooms needed a fire to be habitable, and Holmes insisted that we sit right next to the fire in his.

"I will speak in a whisper," murmured he, "and its crackling will thwart any unwanted listeners."

"The Germans are unclear whether there is one killer or more at loose in the south-eastern part of their city, but I believe it is only one. It is too monstrous a coincidence that two separate killers should strike on the same night within a mile of each other and while Nebe, in particular, is looking to find more than one killer, he has overlooked a communality in the way the train killings are carried out."

I raised my eye-brows in question.

"In all three cases on the train, the woman attacked was in second-class. Either the victim had a second-class ticket, or her attacker had invited her to join him in second class."

"What about Nebe's theory that it is a foreigner living in Berlin?"

"It is obvious nonsense since the attacker is able to converse with his targets before he attacks them, and none has mentioned a foreign accent – indeed Frau Bendorf obviously spoke to a German who had the same everyday concerns as any other German and expressed them like a German would. I would let Nebe waste his time and interview every forced labourer at Wuhlheide, were it not for the risk that, unless his belief that a foreigner is at work is shown to be nonsense, he has both the inclination and the authority to carry out his threat of conducting random exemplary executions. I find myself in the perverse position of wanting to investigate this case to prevent a mass execution of innocents and yet, if I find the killer, I will be assisting Germany's war-effort. Faced with a dilemma such as this I cannot act until I get word from London that I have its permission to do so."

My room was next to that that of Holmes and there was an inter-connecting door. I retired there and engrossed myself in medical reports of some of the prisoners.

I went to light one of my Bradley's cigarettes and found I was out of matches.

I knocked on the inter-connecting door and Holmes bade me enter. He was sitting at a writing desk and turned in his chair to look at me as I entered.

Immediately in front of him were laid out maps of Berlin – some of the city's surface features, and some of the overground and underground railway lines. But lying on the desk to one side was a piece of paper with what looked to be the letters of the alphabet in upper case arranged in a curious circle – some the right way up, some sideways on the page, and some upside down.

Holmes took no particular pains to conceal the page from me, and I knew better than to ask for explanation, particularly when his response to my arrival was to ask, "Well?" with a note of impatience in his voice.

I explained my errand, received some vestas from him, and went back to my own room.

When an hour later I knocked again to bid him good-night, it was to find Holmes sitting cross-legged on his bed, surrounded at his feet by his maps, and at his head, by a haze of pipe tobacco. I returned to my room and was about to go to bed when I felt the urge to look at the papers again. In the end, I sat on the bed to do so. Even if I had gone to bed, I doubt I would have slept as the tobacco Holmes was smoking emanated an unfamiliar warm, almost leathery scent with hints of pepper, tar, and coffee through the door.

I glanced at the clock and saw that it was only half-past-eleven.

I sat up, wondering whether I should try to turn in, when I heard the door to the corridor from my friend's room open. I padded softly to my own room-door, looked into the dimly lit corridor outside to see the back of Holmes, dressed but without a coat, heading away from me. Pausing only to light a cigarette, I stole down the thickly carpeted corridor after him. The distant ding of a bell and the whirring sound of machinery told me he had got into a lift which departed as I walked towards it.

I summoned a lift for myself.

The Adlon hotel is vast, the number of rooms I could obtain access to small, and Holmes had a head-start over me of a minute. I therefore decided to confine my search for Holmes to checking the grandiose reception rooms on the ground floor, as I could go there without too many questions being asked if I were stopped.

All the rooms were unlit but some dim lighting in the corridor meant that they were not in complete darkness. Their doors were open and the fourth room I peered into was the one with the cabinet-gramophone. And that was where Holmes was. But he was completely absorbed in a way that from my vantage point at the entrance to the room I could not understand. The cabinet-gramophone stood against the far wall from the door and Holmes was bent over it, apparently looking at the turntable. Occasionally I thought I could discern him mutter something, but I could not make out what and, in truth, I could not imagine what he was doing.

After much less than a minute, he stood upright and looked intently at his watch.

And then he then bent over the gramophone again, before straightening up once more and casting his eyes towards me standing in the doorway.

But he gave no sign of being aware of my presence – whether he was so engrossed in what he was doing or whether he was in some way temporarily blinded, I had no way of telling, even though I was no more than thirty feet away from him and could see him clearly even in the mere half-light thrown from the dim bulbs in the corridor.

And after a few seconds, he bent once more over the gramophone, before straightening again to look at his watch.

After observing him repeat this about five times, I decided that there was nothing more to learn, returned to my room, and got into bed.

I lay awake waiting for him to return, although whether I would have pressed him on his nocturnal perambulations I could not be sure then and remain unsure now. What I can be sure of is that he had not returned to his room before my ears were assailed by the wail of air-raid sirens. I had not heard such sirens out in Fenny Stratford, but we had been briefed on what to do by Obermann.

From the sounding of sirens, we would, he told us, have a maximum of forty-five minutes before bombs would start to fall assuming that Berlin was the target and assuming it was not a leafleting raid.

I dressed, took up my small, prepacked case with my identity documents, opened it briefly to deposit the packet containing my few remaining Bradley's of Oxford Street cigarettes inside, and headed down to the air-raid shelter under the hotel.

Inasmuch as any air-raid shelter can be luxurious, the Adlon's merited that description. It was large, well lit, and with comfortable seating.

But there was no sign of Holmes as I entered. I sat down and the bombs start to drop. Suddenly there was a loud report of one landing close. The earth shook, and the lights flickered, relit briefly, and then went out. Although no one was hurt, we were in pitch blackness.

Someone lit what I was told subsequently were called Hindenburg lights. These are shallow bowls of tallow with a wick, and I looked around in this meagre of lights that they cast. I could hear voices, and, in the confined space, I could smell sweat and stale breath.

My reader will imagine my sense of re-assurance when someone sat down next to me, a hand touched my sleeve, and a familiar voice whispered, "Ah, Watson, good to see you here. Not a word! The locals may not like giving shelter to British subjects in a British air-raid."

At that point I heard the report of another bomb landing, and then another, and another.

I could hear my other neighbour, a bald-headed, mild-mannered looking man in his late fifties, muttering under his breath.

I listened closely and realised, to my complete surprise, he was counting in English.

"One…two…three… four… five… six… seven…eight," he murmured and then stopped.

There was another series of bomb reports and again I could just make out my neighbour counting up to eight in English.

The process was repeated for about hour and finally came silence before there was another wailing of sirens to give the all-clear. People rose as one to leave the shelter but, almost as soon as he got up, my neighbour collapsed at my side, and lay on the floor clutching his chest.

As a doctor, I felt I had no choice, even in these strange circumstances, but to intervene.

"Ich bin Arzt," I said to the crowd of by-standers and loosened the man's collar. I then listened first to his heart rate, which was normal, and then to his breath, which was also normal. As my ear was poised over my former neighbour's mouth, I heard a faint whisper. "Have me taken to my room, doctor."

"Nur Schock," I told bystanders – relieved that the words in German and English have the same meaning and, with the help of Obermann, Holmes and I conveyed the man to his room on the second floor and laid him on his bed. Obermann went back to his duties and, as soon as he did so, the man sat up.

"It would be hard," said he, "for an Englishman not to recognise Mr Sherlock Holmes and Dr John Watson, even in circumstances as strange as these. The pair of you constitute a single fixed point in a changing world. And I am proud that my act of simulation seems as successful at taking you in, Dr Watson, as the repeated acts of simulation that your friend practises on you. My name may be known to you. I am Pelham Grenville Wodehouse."

PG Wodehouse!

I had known that he had been living as a tax-exile in France but had not given any thought to what might have happened to him after that country's fall to the Germans six months earlier.

"I had been leading a most pleasant existence near Le Touquet," said the writer, "but, unseen in the background, Fate was quietly loading lead into its boxing-glove. I don't remember the exact day when I heard that the Teuton was on the march, but it all happened so quickly. One minute one was wondering whether the whisky had received quite the right amount of emphasis in one's soda, the next a maid was rushing up to inform one that columns of German tanks were advancing down the main street of the next village."

"What did you do?

"As a patriotic Englishman with an English wife, and an English dog, I felt it incumbent on me not to fall into the hands of the enemy and sallied forth in my motor-car with the objective of driving to

Portugal. Alas, my ambition as a driver exceeded that of the engine of my vehicle, which spluttered to a halt within two miles of our starting point, and we had to return on foot. We ventured forth again in a car lent to us by a kind neighbour, but we soon found our path impeded by columns of refugees fleeing the German advance, and we were forced to repair back to Le Touquet."

"What happened next?"

"Further attempt at flight was impossible. I am nearly sixty and even if I had felt able to make what our American cousins refer to as a home run – an expression from baseball, Mr Holmes, which may not be familiar to you – our new German masters were most insistent on the desirability of separating us from our possessions. I was required to report to the local Kommandant every day, and then after spells of what I can only call chokey in various parts of Belgium, I was transported in a cattle truck across to a province called Upper Silesia in the eastern part of Germany."

"How was that?" I asked, spellbound at the narrative that was unfolding.

"Let me confine myself to the observations, Dr Watson, that transport on a cattle truck is something which is fit only for cattle," said the writer, "And, that it pains the sensibilities to think that if there is an Upper Silesia, then even people as limited in deductive powers as you and I, Doctor, can deduce that there must also be a Lower Silesia."

"So how can you afford to live here at the Adlon?" I asked.

"In my own small way, Dr Watson, my works have, like yours, found a favourable reception in Germany, even though the average German is not known for his love of the light-hearted – Hegel and Nietzsche being rather more the sort of thing to which his fancy turns when he is in the mood for a relaxing read. But I sell enough of my works here, that the royalties enable me to live at the Adlon. If I did not have access to those royalties, I might very well find myself back at a civilian internment camp – they call them Ilags, which is a rather amusing term, to distinguish them from Offlags, which are camps for officers, and Stulags, for the lower ranks. I have, I fear, been a lag for all too long."

"I assume, Mr Wodehouse," said my friend, a note of impatience in his voice, although there was nothing else to entertain us at a quarter to six in the morning in wartime Berlin, "that your act of simulation was to avail yourself of my services."

"Mr Holmes," replied Wodehouse, "your presence here in Berlin can only mean some great game is on. I have no knowledge of what it might be, and I have no desire to inquire, but if my freedom could form a part of that game, then I would be eternally grateful."

"My ability to act is highly circumscribed at present," replied my friend, "but I shall bear what you have said in mind."

"The Germans want me to make broadcasts to America. They feel that such broadcasts would show that they are not the brutes portrayed in the British press which is where the Americans get their ideas of the Germans from. I have refused, although I don't think my refusal is doing much for my chances of release."

"Why were you counting in the air-raid shelter?" asked I finally.

"I fear that I fall into the highly select category of Britons who is used to suffering British air-raids. I know that if you hear eight reports from dropped bombs, it means that one 'plane has dropped all its bombs as each bomber has eight bombs in its cradle. So, after the eighth detonation, you know that that 'plane is going to turn for home. Civilised, isn't it?"

The News from London and Switzerland

Seven o'clock Berlin time on the evening of Sunday the 8th of December 1940.

Holmes rotated the dials on the wireless set that Frölicher had given us to get the best signal, although he still kept the wireless at the lowest audible sound level.

In these strangest of circumstances, it was reassuring to hear the bongs of Big Ben chime out and the newsreader intone, "This is the BBC broadcasting from London. Here are the headlines." The bulletin started with references to German bombing raids on London and a north-eastern coastal town, and then moved to discuss the campaign to dislodge the Italian occupying forces from Ethiopia. My reader will understand the impatience with which Holmes and I listened until the bulletin announced it would conclude with a special report on living conditions in Switzerland.

The report was brief and told us nothing that Holmes and I had not observed during our time there, but, as it came to an end, Holmes turned to me and said, "We have got, in these highly unpromising circumstances, good Watson, another case, and it is Dr Joseph Goebbels who is our petitioner."

"It will be my pleasure and honour to work with you once more," I heard myself saying, a thrill in my voice.

"It may be as well if I summarise to you where we are in this case. There have been four attacks on women travelling on or near the same stretch of S-Bahn or Berlin over-ground commuter line. There has also been a killing at a nearby allotment where a woman was a resident. While it is conceivable that there is more than one attacker, the general *modus operandi* appears to be that someone with the air of authority bestowed by a uniform attacks lone women, as they sit in the dimly lit second-class carriage of the train. It has not been clear what the motive for the attack is, but the victims are not robbed. One victim has been the subject of a sexual attack, but the others have not."

"So, you consider three of the four railway attacks to be motiveless?"

"I am unable, shall we say, to find a motive for them unless the attacker is motivated by the thrill he gets from throwing his victim from the train. It may be that that was why Frau Franke was the subject of a savage beating and a sexual attack when the others were not. The short intervals between stations on the German S-Bahn do not allow time for a significant assault, but the attack on her occurred close to the railway line, but not on a train between stations and so her assailant could reckon on a longer time undisturbed."

"Are you able to form any picture of the attacker?"

"Beyond that it is a man who has a uniform, is right-handed, and is a German – characteristics that apply to nine tenths of the male workers on the S-Bahn who are nearly five thousand in number, and does not exclude an outsider, I have none that is of any use in identifying him."

"And how much will you be able to tell Lüdtke?"

"On the information I have, I have no reason to withhold anything from him. For all its complexities, this is a criminal investigation like any other we have been engaged for. I would only choose to withhold information if we came across something useful to Germany's war-effort."

"So, what is your next move to be?"

"The local police have been no more adept at investigating this crime than Lestrade would have been. I will need to see another branch of them. I may use the stratagem I used for Colonel Moran in the matter you chronicled as *The Empty House.*"

"You placed a wax model of your head in the window of our sitting-room at Baker Street, and you caught Colonel Moran when he shot at it with an air-rifle," I replied in some confusion.

"Precisely so, good Watson. There can be no doubt that the strange surroundings we find ourselves in, are causing your talents as a detective to blossom."

Baiting the Trap

Rather to my surprise it was me to whom Frau Friederike Wicking, head of the Women's Criminal Police, chose to address her remarks when I accompanied Holmes and Lüdtke to see her.

"Almost all the females you portray during your narratives, Dr Watson, are both highly capable and extremely beautiful. I hold that this is an entirely unrealistic portrayal of my sex. I have been in charge of my section of the police since 1927, and my women are in the main of, at best, ordinary intelligence, and are frankly dowdy in looks. If that were not the case, they would have able to find husbands and would be looking after his family while he is at the front, as befits a woman, rather than having to work in my force."

The stately, grey-haired woman turned to Lüdtke.

"My women-officers can assist their male superiors with tasks fitting their weaker sex – like comforting women who have been the victims of an assault or performing searches of female suspects. But other than that, I am most reluctant to allow them to take an active part in an investigation – particularly one with the characteristics you have described."

"Frau Wicking," said Lüdtke, "we have had at least three deaths and two major assaults on women on or near the S-Bahn. We must use all our resources to avoid any more. The criminal has a record of striking at women travelling on their own in the second-class compartment of an S-Bahn train at night. When he has reduced his victim to unconsciousness, he throws them from the train."

"And in what way could my female officers help?"

"We would have one sit in second-class to act as a bait to the criminal. When he attacked, the female officer would be equipped with a gun to wound or kill the criminal."

Frau Wicking stared at Lüdtke.

"That would not be possible for a woman. I will not permit members of the Women's Criminal Police to be armed."

"But that is putting any woman officer who works on this case in danger. Surely you must have one who can fire a pistol."

"But none that I will authorise to do so. Can you not organize things so that my officer can signal the need for assistance if she is attacked?"

"The train is dark and loud. If the female officer is to sit on her own, anyone who can assist her must be in the next compartment. How can we devise a signal to bring a male officer to the assistance of one of your women before the assailant overcomes her?"

"That, Herr Lüdtke, is your problem. I have made my final offer. I am prepared to place my women at your disposal on the condition that they are bait. She turned to Holmes, "But I fear I am not prepared to place any of my women at your disposal for them to take any role more active than that of a wax model such as you used in *The Empty House*."

We went back to Lüdtke's office. The inspector was fuming. "She wants to protect her women and yet with what she is proposing she is putting any we take into more danger."

His gaze suddenly fixed on Holmes. "In *The Mazarin Stone*, did you not disguise yourself as a woman with a parasol?"

Holmes gave a rare smile at the recollection. "I hardly think at my advanced age that such an approach is practical for the present investigation."

"But," said Lüdtke, "given the flaws in the plan we have formulated with Frau Wicking, an armed male officer dressed as a woman and travelling alone might be a sensible adjunct to what we propose to do."

As my reader may imagine, finding in the Germany of 1940 a male officer prepared to dress as a female to act as a bait for a multiple murderer, was a difficult task.

In the end we chose a short, thin man – Heinrich Torgauer – of forty-one years.

He was fitted out in a hardened hat, gloves to conceal his masculine hands, and knee-high boots. I confess that even in the dusk with the light behind him, he would not have fooled me that he was a woman for a second, but I have pointed out the dimness of the second class-carriage of an S-Bahn train.

As our female decoy, Frau Wicking had identified a Fräulein Claudia Brunner who was also given a protective hat. She was a tall woman in her early thirties with a determined jut to her jaw.

So it was that Torgauer, dressed as a woman, as well as Brunner, Nebe, Lüdtke, four additional male officers, all dressed in plain clothes, plus Holmes, and I met at Rummelsburg Station at 10 o'clock on the night of the 12th of December.

"It could be a long night," said Lüdtke, a note of gloom in his voice.

Holmes rubbed his hands together. *"The Speckled Band, The Hound of the Baskervilles, The Six Napoleons,"* he recalled with glee. "They all involved a long wait. But all had the fairly certain expectation that our wait would be rewarded on the first night we staged a vigil. I would say that the chances of our criminal striking tonight are no more than one in twenty based on his past record, and with three operating trains on this line that means that the chances of us finding anything are one in sixty."

"We are on this train every night till Christmas," responded Lüdtke slightly defensively. "To evade us, our criminal must either not strike, which would be of itself a result, or be consistently lucky. We, by contrast, need only be lucky once to catch him."

Trains on the S-Bahn have five sections.

There is one third-class section at each end and one in the middle. Between each of the three third-class sections, are two much smaller second-class sections. Torgauer and Brunner each took a place in one of the second-class sections while the rest of our party split into the third-class carriages at the ends of the train. I sat with Lüdtke and two officers, while Holmes sat with the other two officers at the other end of the train.

It was wearisome work sitting in wait in the dimmest of lighting on a run-down S-Bahn train. As the night wore on, the number of passengers dwindled, although there were always enough people sitting in third-class to justify the running of the train through the night, as the effect of wartime shift patterns became visible just as the black-out swallowed everything else up.

Lüdtke became more and more agitated as the time passed. "I've got to catch him!" he whispered in German to me.

His cigarette-end glowed scarlet through the gloom and his sucking in of the smoke was quite audible, so hard did he pull on the butt. He gave a wary glance at the other two officers. "I can speak English well," he said, "and I'll take the chance that they can't. Before the National Socialist party came to power, it was my job to keep the party's activities under surveillance and investigate when I saw fit. They were an illegal organization and into every sort of crime – general thuggery, theft, extortion, vandalism. I fought them tooth and nail. And I had a string of successes in other fields too. When the National Socialists came to power, they wanted to throw me out, but I got another job in the criminal police. There are many who'd like to get rid of me still, and they will use this as the reason if I don't sort it out."

I had not anticipated Lüdtke confiding his personal situation to me but there was nothing else to do as the train rattled between stations, so I leant forward to hear what he had to say.

"I don't have connections in the party. I only joined this year when it was made clear to me that failure to do so would be disastrous for my career. I am in the eight millions."

"Eight millions?"

"My party member number tells anyone who wants to know when I joined the party. Nebe joined in 1930 so his party number is in the late eight-hundred-thousands. It is no wonder that he has risen so high. He believes in what the party is doing."

"I fear he believes in it only too fervently."

"People like me, who applied to join the party after it came to power, by contrast, are seen as opportunists. For a long time, we were not allowed to join at all."

The night of the 10th of December passed without incident, and so did the next few nights. By day I was still assessing prisoners-of-war – Goebbels had already accepted applications for one-hundred-and-fifty to be returned home. It was the early morning of Sunday the 22nd of December that our luck changed, although I admit that I have had to check my diary to confirm the date to such an extent did short daylight hours, blackout, and travelling the same stretch of line over and over again, make me lose track of time.

We had boarded a Schnell-Bahn train at half-past nine the previous evening.

With two second-class sections on the train, we had again split our ambuscade into two and this time Holmes, Lüdtke, and I sat together in the dim light of third class.

With so much watching and waiting, it was inevitable that we should engage in conversation even though it might warn any would be assailant that our group of travellers consisted of people acquainted with each other. And with so much manpower dedicated to the hunt of the killer, and nothing to show for it, apart perhaps from the lack of another killing, it was also inevitable that Lüdtke should be showing signs of the strain he was under.

"If there is another one, I don't know what they will do to me," he said, his cigarette end again glowing red.

"Do you think that the killer knows that there is a police presence on the line?" I asked.

"Perhaps," said Lüdtke in a non-committal voice. "You don't know who is on your side and who is watching and waiting for you to fail."

"Do you really think, my dear Lüdtke," countered Holmes, "that a regime such as this needs to find a reason to get rid of you? If Nebe wants you out, he would go ahead and do it. And do you think he would undermine the investigation by talking loosely about your attempts to catch the criminal."

Lüdtke leant back in his seat.

"When Hitler was born there were three fairies present. One promised him that all Germans would be honest, one that they would all be intelligent, and one that they would all be National Socialists. And then another fairy came and said that Germans would only have two out of those three qualities. You can think about the people you have met and decide for yourself who falls into which category. At this rate, I may be unique among Germans in only having honesty as a quality because my idea of staking out the trains seems to have got us…"

At that moment we heard a shrill whistle from the second-class department.

We dashed for the dividing door – Holmes, belying his years, and Lüdtke at the front of our party.

As we entered the carriage, a blast of icy air struck our faces, and told us that a passenger door had been opened. And framed by the doorway with its open door was Fräulein Brunner wrestling desperately with a man. The man glanced up from the struggle as we entered. And then, even above the roar of the train, there was a crashing noise.

Brunner's assailant had leapt from the speeding train onto the clinker below and disappeared out of view.

Lüdtke ran to the door that was still hanging open.

It says much for his courage, that his immediate reaction to events was to make to leap out of it. A junior colleague had to wrap his arms around him – if we had been in England, I would have described the colleague's action as a rugby tackle – and for a second Lüdtke's legs kicked at thin air outside while his colleague held him in his grip. I confess I think that if Lüdtke had indeed jumped out of the moving train, then Holmes, for all that he was in his eighty-seventh year, would have followed him. As it was, my friend had the presence of mind to pull the emergency cord.

The brakes screamed on immediately, but it took the train what turned out later to be half a mile to grind to a halt.

"If he's dead or incapacitated from his fall, we've got him," exclaimed Lüdtke as he dropped down onto the side of the track. "But if he's been as lucky with his landing as two of his victims were, we have no chance of even getting close."

We joined him and walked back up the track flashing our torches with their limited beam onto the ground.

"As part of a police enquiry, we can shine torches as long as the air-raid sirens do not sound," said Lüdtke, when I questioned whether this was permitted.

But we found no sign of Brunner's assailant.

"We will have to wait until it is light to do a proper forensic search," said Lüdtke gloomily, as we walked along the clinker.

We had by now reached a station – Hirschgarten by name.

"It means stag garden," said Lüdtke. "We're within fifteen kilometres of the centre of Berlin but it's quite rural here. The killer has escaped. There's a café over there that stays open all night. Let us take stock of where we are on the case before we go back to conduct a detailed examination. I would welcome your thoughts Mr Holmes."

We entered through the black-out curtains and Lüdtke placed a call to his station to give a situation-report and to say where we were.

The café's interior was smoke-filled, for all that it was almost empty of customers. "It's fifty pfennigs for a coffee made from coffee beans and thirty pfennigs if it is made from acorns," the waitress said, I think slightly taken aback at the arrival of such a large party at half-past-five in the morning.

Out of curiosity, I ordered an acorn coffee, which in the dim light – all that was allowed in the café – looked quite like the real thing, but which had a taste that only hinted of coffee and left behind the bitterest of aftertastes.

"For enhanced concentration, I will need a normal coffee," Holmes had said, and drank from the cup when it was brought without saying anything.

"So near and yet so far!" groaned Lüdtke.

"I fear," said I, "that it may be some time before the criminal strikes again – at least on the S-Bahn. He looks to have got away, and he will now realise that the railway is a trap."

At that moment our waitress approached us.

"Is one of you gentlemen called Lüdtke?"

"I am."

"There's an urgent call for you, sir."

It was only a minute before Lüdtke came back.

"There's been another woman's body found," he exclaimed. "It's two stops down the line but the trains are now not going any further than the next station so we will have to walk from there."

The dawn had turned the sky a steely grey by the time we had got to Friedrichshagen, and the body was most of the way down the track to the next station.

The line ran quite straight, and in the distance we could see a party of people to the left of the track, whom I took to be railway staff come to ensure that no one tampered with the body.

"It could be a suicide," said Lüdtke, I think with a note of slightly forlorn hope in his voice. "Just before Christmas is a time when suicides are at a peak."

"I assume that is her handbag there," replied Holmes, sharp-eyed as ever, as he pointed to a black clutch-bag just visible in a bush by the left side of the track. "It is surely too monstrous a coincidence that a handbag belonging to someone else should be found at a time and a place where a woman's body is found. The body came from a train coming in our direction, so this handbag has been thrown out after the body had left the train. This is definitely another murder with the same pattern of the killer ejecting his victim and throwing out her possessions after her."

"Hit over the head with a heavy blunt object," I confirmed grimly as we stood over the bloodied victim at the crime scene a few minutes later. She lay by the track, her fall having left her limbs contorted into completely unnatural positions.

"Time of death?" Lüdtke asked me.

"She has been dead for no more than two hours and probably less. The blood from her head has hardly congealed."

Lüdtke lit a cigarette.

When he had smoked it right down to the stub, he used it to light a second one, and he was half-way through this second cigarette before he spoke again.

"You mean he has struck again so soon after we had nearly caught him?" he ground out in the end.

"Assuming there is only one killer, I can read this no other way."

"What nerve! He has been ambushed and leaps from a moving train to get away. Yet he strikes again within the hour."

"A killer may be as exhilarated by a near escape from capture as by a killing," I said thoughtfully.

"What do you make of this, Herr Holmes?"

"Where are the financial and personnel records of the Schnell-Bahn maintained?"

"They are at the offices of the Reichsbahn, the company that controls all the railway companies in Germany," replied Lüdtke. "I have had people go through them looking for suspects, but the number of employees is too big to make narrowing down suspects a worthwhile exercise when we have no features to distinguish our killer."

"Then your only alternative is to question thousands of railway staff and see whether you get a consensus on possible suspects from your questions. With five thousand employees, that will be no small undertaking."

It was lunchtime on the 22nd of December when we arrived back at the Adlon Hotel and, waiting for us in the reception, was Herr Frölicher.

"I have an urgent message from London for you," he said. "This was telegrammed to Berne and then from Berne to here. I have brought it straight round."

"Does that not mean that the Germans will probably know its contents?" I asked.

Frölicher shrugged.

"That is the risk your masters have taken."

"I am sure we are being recalled if London has no desire to keep the matter a secret," said Holmes, tearing open the envelope. He handed the message to me, and I read out.

"'RETURN TO LONDON AT ONCE STOP ANTHONY EDEN NOW FOREIGN SECRETARY'"

"I fear, Inspector," said Holmes, "that I am now highly restricted in what I can say to you."

My readers will perhaps understand that leaving Berlin for London in wartime at Christmas was no easy matter to organise, even for people with diplomatic status, as documents needed to be obtained and permissions sought. It will perhaps also not surprise them to learn that, even in these circumstances, Christmas Day spent with Sherlock Holmes was in every sense much like any other day spent with Sherlock Holmes. Thus, I have nothing to add to the foregoing narrative until the morning of Sunday the 29th of December.

On that morning we sat in a reception room at the Adlon as we had had to leave our rooms, and our train from Berlin had been delayed by an air-raid. We were thus barred from any form of investigative activity, barred from any work on the prisoner exchange, and unable, at least until an alternative routing was found for our train to Geneva, to leave Berlin. Although we were not in any conventional sense combatants in the conflict, it is hard to imagine a better illustration of the aphorism that war is ninety per cent tedium and ten per cent terror.

Suddenly Lüdtke entered.

"There's been another one!" he exclaimed.

I am not sure that Holmes should have shown any interest at all in the circumstances we found ourselves, but my friend stirred himself.

"Pray speak," said he. "I may not respond in any way, but any mental stimulation is welcome in this intellectual vacuum."

"I have had officers ride the train in the early morning as well as late at night. But it has got me nowhere. This morning at Karlshorst Station – "

"The same station as where the first two deaths occurred?"

"Precisely so. A Mrs Gertrud Sievert was attacked..."

"How similar was the attack to the other attacks?"

Lüdtke sighed.

"Like the last attack, the victim was attacked on a train on the south-eastern part of the S Bahn. She was thrown out of the moving train, we estimate just after half-past-six this morning, having sustained a heavy blow to the head from a blunt implement. Her body was found at half past eight. Further down the track from the direction of travel were found her handbag and her umbrella"

"Was there any evidence of what class of travel she was using."

Lüdtke sighed again.

"It was second class."

"No witnesses? No traces of the killer?"

"We are still investigating but have turned up nothing so far."

"I do not believe I am exceeding the limits of what I am allowed to do if I say that the main features of each successive case replicate those of the previous ones. Were there no features at all to distinguish this from the others?"

"There were none. The killer's last two victims have both been killed in the hours of darkness on a Schnell-Bahn train in the south-east of Berlin. The only event amongst the two assaults and the four murders that was in any way different was that of Irmgard Freese, who was not attacked on a train, but whose attack was within sight of the same stretch of tracks where all these attacks have been made."

"There is nothing so featureless as the commonplace. A truism in itself."

A Debrief and a Rebrief

"So, Mr Holmes, I have no idea why you felt you should help the Germans to investigate this matter in any way at all."

On our return to Britain, by the same wearisome route that we had had to follow on the way to Berlin, we had been summoned once more to the Foreign Office. Anthony Eden glowered at us from behind his desk. Normally I give a description of the characters when I introduce them for the first time, but with his trim moustache and light colouring, the person whom Eden, who is pictured on the cover of this work, resembled most was me as I had looked perhaps forty years previously.

"Foreign Secretary, I had been given the brief of negotiating a prisoner exchange. As Mr Butler himself had said, we had very few prisoners of our own to give the Germans in return as we have taken very few prisoners of our own. I obtained permission from the Foreign Office for what I did, and I can only assume the matter went before Lord Halifax."

"Well, now that Mr Churchill has seen fit to send Lord Halifax to Washington to represent this country there, we will have no parleying with the enemy of any sort."

"So, no attempts will be made to repatriate prisoners or to make life more bearable for them? And we run the risk that the Germans will string up some innocent prisoners if they cannot find the true killer on their railway network."

"Our prisoners' welfare, we will leave to the Swiss and the Red Cross. The risk of the Germans dispensing summary justice is one we can do nothing about, although it reinforces my desire to see this war through to its conclusion. I resigned over the settlement the present Prime Minister's predecessor, Neville Chamberlain, reached with our enemies and came back into government to sort out the mess it created once Mr Chamberlain had gone. I can see no role for you in this, Mr Holmes, and I wish you and Dr Watson a good day."

And that seemed to be the end of our adventure.

A few prisoners repatriated as a result of Holmes's initial work on the S-Bahn case was all we had to show for it. We returned to Fenny Stratford and our life, lived in shades of black, brown, and grey, carried on. I tried to vary our diet of bread and potatoes by doing more work on the vegetable garden, although I knew that it would bring no benefit till the autumn harvest, while Holmes focused on his bees.

The war continued on its course and almost none of it seemed to work in my country's favour.

It was one morning in late March that there was a knock on the door. I answered it to be faced by a uniformed driver.

"I have instructions to take Mr Holmes to London. I regret, Dr Watson, that I was explicitly told that your presence is not required."

Although, for obvious reasons, I have not in my previous narratives dwelt on instances where I was excluded from Holmes's cases, this was not such an unusual event in the annals of our co-operation, particularly when matters of state were involved. After Holmes had gone, I spent the day digging the vegetable plot, and he returned just as it was getting dark.

"I cannot tell you my whole brief," said he, "but we have been charged with going back to Berlin to try and persuade the Germans to release more prisoners, and to apprehend this killer on the trains."

"We?"

"Yes, they tried to persuade me to go on my own, but I was adamant that that my task would be rendered easier by the presence of someone reliable with both medical and military experience, and whose absence would not mean that frontline position was unmanned. You were the obvious candidate."

I could at this point give my reader another account of the perils of a wartime commercial flight but instead I will recount an incident that occurred on our journey which was to assume ever more importance as the events progressed.

Rather to my surprise, we were again told that transport would be provided to us to get us from Fenny Stratford to Whitchurch. When the black car arrived, sitting in it was a was a brisk, uniformed member of the Women's Auxiliary Air-Force or WAAF who introduced herself to us as Woman-Officer Oliver.

"I have been detailed to join you gentlemen on your journey to Bristol," said she, "but I cannot tell you why until we get there."

After a long and tedious drive, we passed through the formalities in the airport building at all times under Oliver's watchful eye.

"The in-bound 'plane to take you to Lisbon," she disclosed at last, "is flying in from Reykjavík."

I vaguely knew that Iceland had been under British control since May of the previous year, but I had no idea what that had to do with us.

"On board the 'plane," continued Oliver, "is the new United States Ambassador to Britain, John Gilbert Winant. We couldn't tell the press of the arrival of the new ambassador for reasons of security but, if I introduce you to him, Dr Watson, could you ask him to say a few words which will be relayed to the press for publication in today's papers? Your word will in any case carry far more authority than that of any journalist. You and Mr Holmes can then go on your way."

The 'plane could only land in the dark and, though we heard it arrive, we did not see anything of the new ambassador until he was in the airport building.

When I was finally introduced to him, it did not require Holmes's eye to know that the tall, well-dressed, and coiffed diplomat had known in the United States none of the privations to which we had become accustomed in Britain. I was unsure what mood he would be in after leaving the comfort of his home country, being subjected to a hazardous six-hour flight, and then being interviewed in a makeshift blacked-out airport building, but Winant shook Holmes and me warmly by the hand.

"I'm very glad to be here," he declared. "There is no place I'd rather be at this time than in England. And to be met by Sherlock Holmes and Dr Watson – fixed points in a changing world – goes beyond my wildest dreams." The first sentence – natural modesty precluded me repeating the second, although Holmes may not have been quite so reticent – were to appear on the front page of every British newspaper, and Winant continued, "I would not be here, if I did not have the President's trust, and he will take account in his actions of what I say," but Holmes and I were already in Portugal when the new ambassador's words were published.

Little had changed since our previous sojourn – "our fighters, barrage balloons, and flack towers saw off your bombers," Lüdtke told us, and it was certainly the case that there had been no increase in the number of damaged buildings. "Destroying an enemy capital, as we ourselves seem to be finding, is no easy task."

I had expected events to follow a similar course as they had done in the winter. And indeed, I was kept busy during the day, as I visited prisoners-of-war and ranking them in order of need and ability to make the hazardous journey home. But at night I slept in my bed and of Holmes I saw almost nothing. He was gone when I ate my meagre breakfast in the morning and did nothing but smoke in the evening. To my surprise, he took a huge interest in the local press, and surrounded himself with German newspapers. My knowledge of German was sufficient to see that they all carried the same, I assumed by no means inaccurate, message of military success – Yugoslavia and Greece were the latest conquests – derived from communiqués and could not see how reading them in detail was of help to my friend. There were no ambuscades to the S-Bahn. The only disclosure Holmes made to me of what he was doing was, "I swapped my food stamps for Obermann's tobacco, good Watson. I am on a mission where concentration is the alpha and omega while digestion merely saps the body of energy." Our rations were so meagre, his abstinence from food seemed to have no affect on his thin frame.

We still had adjoining rooms and it was on the night of Monday the 28th of April that I was shaken awake. Behind my friend I could see Wodehouse.

"Come Watson! The game is afoot! The stakes have never been higher!"

"Where are we going?"

"All will become clear to you. I have taken the case as far as I can, and it is now time to make what Mr Wodehouse here previously referred to as a home run."

He turned to Wodehouse.

"Now Mr Wodehouse, if you would make your way through the front entrance of the hotel, I have prevailed upon Obermann to overlook your irregular departure. If you go to the Brandenburg Gate, you will be approached by two Berlin cabbies. Pay no heed to the overtures of the first one, but step into the cab of the second one, who will take you to our rendezvous."

"And you will not tell me what that is?"

"I fear I cannot, but the driver will know it."

"And you cannot come with me now."

"I fear that the three of us leaving the hotel together might attract too much attention and there are a number of matters on which I require Dr Watson's assistance."

I am not sure if Wodehouse was convinced by my friend's instructions, but he left us, and I readied myself.

"Where are we heading for?" I asked. "Can you tell me?"

"We are heading east, my friend."

"More time on the south-eastern S-Bahn?"

"I think you will find the journey a good deal longer than any trip on the S-Bahn"

"You make it sound as though the S-Bahn case is a closed matter. What time is it?"

"Half-past ten. Our train leaves at half-past-midnight."

"Are we leaving Berlin altogether?"

"Pray do not tarry in discussions, good doctor. Dress as for our unmissed night-time S-Bahn ambuscades."

I did not need long. Once in the dimly lit corridor, rather than heading for the lift, Holmes took the stairs, and rather than exiting through the hotel lobby, we departed through the kitchens at the rear. "Not the most glamourous exit," said he, as we stepped out into the inky blackness.

Even though I was used to the black-out, I would not have undertaken to find anything in Berlin, but Holmes was as sure-footed as he been back in his Baker Street heyday. And we were in for a long walk. How far was it? I could only follow Holmes by the sound of his footsteps. An hour and ten minutes by my phosphorescent watch, and Holmes suddenly stopped. I heard the sound of wires being cut and then felt my sleeve being grabbed.

I followed the direction in which I was bidden. And then I heard the chuffing of a train. So, was this to be another nocturnal train ride but with our train this time pulled by a steam locomotive?

But the train went past.

After it had gone Holmes whispered.

"By my watch, it is twenty-five minutes past midnight. Our train is due now. Do not ask any questions and do as I say."

I felt myself nodding even though Holmes could not see me.

All I could hear was a peculiar rustling sound.

Then, suddenly, Holmes struck a match.

In that instant I saw to my astonishment a large pile of newspapers to which my friend applied the flame.

"It will be a pleasure to see all of these going up in smoke after having to conceal them in my clothing," he commented, just as I heard the approaching roar of a train, and then a screech of brakes. The locomotive driver was stopping to investigate the blaze.

"Now!" hissed Holmes, "now!" and clutched my sleeve. We mounted the darkened train by the first carriage. The corridor was dimly lit. "Into the first empty compartment," he whispered, when we were on board. "This is a first-class carriage and so there is a fair chance we will find one."

He struck another match. "And now under the seats."

This was a big thing to ask for a man in his eighties, even in good physical condition.

"And not a word until I say," I heard hissed from under the seats on the other side of the compartment. "No tobacco, no movement, no noise."

After a few minutes, with a whistle and a hiss, the train started again.

Given our stop-start journeys from Lisbon to Geneva, and then again up to Berlin – the routes mutilated by the after-effects of the Spanish civil war, and British air attacks on the French and German railway networks – it was striking how smooth our journey was. It had not occurred to me to ascertain what sort of train it was that we had boarded or where it was going, and it was to be several hours before it got light.

It was well into the morning before the train halted. I listened out for station announcements and could make out "Warschau", the German for what had been the Polish capital. So, we were heading east. And another three hours saw us arrive at Brest-Litovsk which I knew to be at the border of the territory that now formed the German Reich and the Soviet Union. It was only once we were across the border that Holmes emerged from under the seat and signalled that I should come out too.

"We have at least another eight hours to go."

"To go? Where are we going?"

"We are going to Moscow, my friend."

As I digested this, the door of our compartment opened, and the conductor entered. I think he was surprised to see anyone and said "Passport" with what I assume was a Russian accent.

Holmes responded in German of which the conductor, as might be expected of someone on the line from Berlin to Moscow, had some knowledge. Holmes handed the conductor his passport, and I could make out him saying, "I am Sherlock Holmes. We are travelling on diplomatic passports. We have an urgent message for Comrade Stalin."

An instant look of recognition crossed the conductor's face at the mention of my friend's name. He pointed to me, and said, "Dr Watson?"

At my nod, he saluted to Holmes and withdrew, only to return half an hour later bearing a venerable looking samovar. "Chai?" he asked solicitously and after our long and uncomfortable confinement under the seats a cup of tea was more than welcome.

It was still over seven hundred miles to Moscow, and it was actually early the following morning that we started to move through that city's suburbs. They were lit, a welcome sight after the dark nights of Berlin, but only dimly.

Holmes had told me nothing of our mission, but, once our diplomatic accreditation had smoothed our progress through Moscow's main station, we got into a taxi, and were on our way to the Kremlin. The presentation of Holmes's card to one of the guards sped us through the entrance and it was not long before we were in an opulent reception-room.

After a few minutes, Stalin, General Secretary of the Soviet Communist party, entered dressed in a plain olive-green uniform and smoking from a bitter smelling pipe. He was accompanied only by a formal-looking interpreter.

To my surprise, before any conversations started, Stalin embraced both Holmes and me, and, as is the custom among men in this part of Eastern Europe, proceeded to bestow fervent kisses on both of us, which I felt I had no choice but to endure. The pen of Mr Wodehouse may have been required to do the scene proper justice, and I will confine myself to the remark that I was grateful that I had already reached my eighty-sixth year before I submitted myself to the experience, although Holmes seemed to treat the embraces as being part of a day's work. It was a while before we had sat down round a table to speak, but I repeat our discussions below as the interpreter relayed them between us.

"Comrade Holmes," began the Soviet leader, "of-course I know your name, and that of Doctor Watson as well. You are someone, Mr Holmes, whom I have always wanted to meet for I regard you as a revolutionary hero and a kindred spirit. It is surely no co-incidence that it is the 1st of May, the time to celebrate the holiday of Labour, that you come to my door."

This was not, I think, quite the response to our arrival from the Soviet leader that my friend had been anticipating, but, as though to avoid a silence, Stalin continued in explanation.

"I admit, Comrade Holmes, that I have read only your early adventures." He shrugged apologetically and continued. "You will understand that being the leader of a party committed to world revolution is a little bit more than a full-time job, so the time I can dedicate to reading is very limited. Thus, your latter works are a pleasure yet to be discovered. But I note that at the beginning of *A Study in Scarlet*, your first clients included a fashionably dressed young girl, a seedy looking pedlar, a slip-shod elderly lady, and a railway porter. It is these people who are denied access to justice by the enemies of the class struggle. And it is you who bring it to them often dispensing it in your own way."

How Holmes felt at being designated a hero of the class struggle by its principal living proponent is unclear to me, but Stalin was by no means finished in his analysis.

"And in *The Noble Batchelor* you comment that your most interesting correspondence comes from the meanest classes of society, and you identify the noble bachelor of the title as grasping and disloyal. And then you neglect to collect a fee from him while choosing to impose your own solution to his problem, just as I choose to impose my own solutions to my nation's problems."

"My correspondence, as I commented at the time," said Holmes, a little insecurely, "has always had the merit of variety, and my cases likewise. And my work has always been its own reward."

At these words Stalin embraced Holmes again, before he turned his gaze to me.

"And you Comrade Watson, are the brave communicator of the class struggle. Without your ardent advocacy of your friend, his noble contribution to it would have passed unremarked. I too, am in my own way, a man of letters although that also has had to be sacrificed to conducting the revolution. Were it not for that, my Georgian poetry might have spread round the world in the same way as your chronicles of your friend's work."

There was a long silence before the Soviet leader spoke again.

"Please feel free to smoke, gentlemen," said he at last, raising his pipe as though in a toast. "I suspect that if you have come all the way from Berlin to speak to me, it will be more than what you refer to in *The Red-Headed League* as a three-pipe problem that you have to present."

"General Secretary, my journey from Berlin was made to warn you that the Germans plan an immediate invasion."

I noted our interpreter's eyebrows rise in alarm as he heard Holmes's warning of an imminent invasion.

Stalin, for his part, shrugged.

"My dear Mr Holmes, I have had one diplomatic delegation after another from your country trying to lure me into an alliance against my country's new German friends. Sending you here is, I am sure, really just another throw of the dice by your government. And no less implausible than the others. I am, shall we say, disappointed, that a hero of labour like you should have allowed himself to have become involved in something like this."

He puffed at his pipe.

"General Secretary, with a starting point of my journey in Berlin, I am better placed than any other Briton to state with confidence that a German invasion of the Soviet Union is imminent."

"The Germans buy millions of roubles worth of raw materials from us which would cost them far more if they bought them elsewhere, if they were able to get them at all. Their whole war-effort is based on it. We have a reputation as a reliable partner, and we are a big empty country with a large army. Why would they be interested in invading us when they have so much from us already and are committing so much to supporting our military efforts?"

"Everyone, General Secretary, imposes his own system as far as his army can reach. Look at the extent of your country. You and your predecessors were not obliged to extend its boundaries in the way they did. But you had the means to extend them, had enemies you reasoned you could defeat, and you chose to attack them. The Germans have the means, will have seen your country's struggles to subdue eastern Poland and Finland, and based on their recent history, it would be surprising indeed if they did not also choose to attack you."

Stalin looked somewhat taken by my friend's analysis.

"What evidence do you have?"

"I have spent the last two weeks examining the planned work schedules of the Reichsbahn or the German railways. Their drivers are scheduled for such a number of journeys to the eastern extremity of the part of Poland that they occupy…"

"You mean to the territory to the west of the Soviet frontier that your government has yet to recognise..," interjected Stalin fiercely.

"…over the next two weeks, that it can only be explained by the moving of a colossal army with all its equipment."

"Mr Holmes, your country is at war with Germany. Why would you be in Berlin looking at the plans of their railway workers?"

"General Secretary, I cannot betray the workings of diplomacy, but I can assure you of the truth of what I am saying about locomotive driver shift patterns."

"Truthful diplomacy," sneered the Soviet leader. "It is like wooden iron or dry water. It does not exist. Everyone is seeking to manipulate me for their own ends. I know to deal with such attempts in my own country so that I need fear no retaliation." He paused, and the menace of his remarks hung in air. "But I am more circumscribed by what I do with my foreign enemies."

He paused and drew heavily on his pipe and asked, this time in a voice suddenly sounding less secure, "Do you have any other evidence?"

"I would put that question back to you. Have there been any notable diplomatic activities from the Germans? Have there been any incursions at the border?"

The Soviet leader looked even less sure of himself.

"The Germans have reduced their diplomatic presence here in Moscow," he said after a pause. "Their ambassador, von der Schulenburg, says fewer staff are needed because relations between our countries are on such a stable footing. And, of course, the 1st of May is a holiday for the National Socialists as well as for us Communists so diplomats will have taken the opportunity for a visit home, even in wartime."

"Anything else?"

"There have also been lots of reports of German 'planes overflying our territory. We have protested but such incursions are nothing new."

"During the day or at night?"

"Both."

"What might German 'planes be doing flying over Soviet controlled air-space, General Secretary?"

"They may be overflying Soviet territory as the shortest route between two pieces of German territory. That is what they have said."

"Flying across land controlled by you…"

"Land that is part of our country," snapped Stalin. "The British will one day soon come to recognise our western borders. The border as it now stands was awarded to us by your foreign secretary, Lord Curzon, in 1919. It moved eastwards later only after our war with Poland. Are you saying I am less of a Soviet than your Lord Curzon was…"

"…by day enables the Germans to see Soviet troop dispositions and flying by night enables them to check Soviet preparedness for operations carried out in darkness."

There was a long silence and the acrid smoke from Stalin's pipe assaulted our nostrils as the tobacco in its bowl turned an angry orange.

"When do you think will they strike?" he asked at last, his voice now no more than a whisper.

"I obtained access to the driver rosters for German occupied Poland three nights ago. Activity has been building since mid-April and remains at a constant level after the 10th of May. The rosters have not yet been drawn up for June. The Germans will have preparations to make on the ground, but they will not want their troops standing idly by or to give you any more time to discover their plans. Surprise is key. I would expect them to attack before dawn on one of the days of the week commencing the 12th of May."

"I have always thought that war between the Soviet Union and Germany was inevitable," mused Stalin, "but I was hoping to delay it until we were better prepared. Do you think I should shoot down their 'planes when they fly over our territories?"

"General Secretary, I fear you must decide your strategy. In the eyes of the world, it might be seen as a provocation."

"What do I care for the eyes of the world?"

"It will be easier to gain support from other countries if you are attacked than if you are perceived as having provoked an attack. There will be plenty of people round the world who would be prepared to join the Germans to fight a war against the Soviet Union and would regard the downing of a German 'plane which had strayed into Soviet airspace as being a just reason for joining the Germans in a war to defeat Bolshevism."

"We Soviets have always stood on our own," retorted Stalin fiercely. "We have in the past fought wars against all our neighbours to get to our rightful place on this planet. We have no need for help from anyone else now. It is a source of pride to me that we have no allies and our only desire if to be left alone. We believe in inevitable world revolution, but my people are discovering the joys of revolution in one country before the rest of the world joins us in the next stage of the ascent of man."

He paused to knock out his pipe and recharged it before continuing.

"We have the Commercial Treaty with the Germans by which we sell them raw material in exchange for weapons, hard currency, and know-how. As a result, their factories supply us with equipment and expertise for our Red Army with the same priority as they offer their own forces. It will be interesting to see what our two great powers, working in a spirit of cold-blooded realism, might achieve. And, if not," he shrugged, "we will see what we can achieve on our own."

He stared ahead and then, suddenly, the Soviet leader looked plaintively at us and asked.

"So is your advice to do nothing until they attack?"

"I would refer you to my previous answer. I can advise you of what is planned by the Germans, but I cannot advise you on a matter of Soviet statecraft."

"Very well. We will announce we plan military exercises, although we will stress that they are for training purposes only. And we shall impose a black-out across our territory. If the Germans ask us why we impose the black-out, we will tell them that it is a cost-saving measure. Our nights are short at this time of year and anyone out in hours of darkness is either out on state business," he paused, "or up to no good. And that at least I know how to deal with."

"Is there anything else you will require from me?"

"My dear Mr Holmes, you cannot imagine I will let you go so easily. I do not know if you are in diplomatic earnest or whether you are laying a diplomatic trap. We will keep you here in Moscow to see how matters develop. If the Germans invade, I will find a way to let you leave the country. And if they do not, well, I am sure the British will see it is in their interests to recover you. On my terms. Or not."

"We are travelling on diplomatic passports."

"And does the British Embassy know where you are here?"

Silence.

"Quite so. If what you say is true, no one knows you are here as you have made your way here from Berlin entirely on your own initiative. And if what you say is false...." The threat in the Soviet leader's words hung in the air.

We were housed in Moscow's Hotel Metropol.

This establishment was not unlike the Adlon in Berlin although our situation was completely different. At the Adlon, we were allowed and expected to go out. At the Metropol, we had adjoining rooms and, at the door of each, was stationed a burly soldier.

My reader may understand the peculiarity of our situation.

The likeliest way we would be able to return to Great Britain was if the most potent army in Europe launched what was intended to be a surprise attack on the world's largest country. If it did not, our fate was in the hands of Joseph Stalin. And, even if the attack did take place, and our country, seeing the National Socialists as a bulwark against the threat of Communism, chose to side with the Germans, I could not be sure we would ever again be welcome on Britain's shores.

Holmes seemed to regard our situation with complete equanimity as we sat with our pipes.

"In the circumstances, it is perhaps inappropriate to quote Martin Luther, but I can do nothing else other than to stand my ground," he said to me one mid-morning. We had not much else to do than to smoke. My friend was deprived of his beehives, his violin, and his chemistry equipment, which might otherwise have kept him occupied. "I am the mere mouthpiece of events over which I have no control," he continued.

"Cassandra was also the mere mouthpiece of events over which she had no control," responded I, full of foreboding. "Her fate was to be right about everything and to be disbelieved by everyone. As I recall, it did not have a happy outcome for her."

At that moment, the door of our room flew open.

In came Stalin accompanied by a soldier with a pistol pointing towards us. It emerged that the soldier spoke some rather guttural English so the dialogue that followed was interpreted by him.

"Dr Watson," said the Soviet leader, "I have taken some time to read some of your accounts of your friend's later adventures."

I was not sure how to react to this gambit and held my counsel.

"I find your friend's last dated criminal case a very telling one in the class struggle."

"Which case are you referring to?" I asked.

"The *Priory School* mentions 1902 as being in the past and there is no dated case thereafter apart from *His Last Bow* of 1914 which is hardly a criminal case."

"That is so," I said cautiously.

Stalin turned to Holmes.

"In *The Priory School* you apprehend Reuben Hayes, the man who kidnapped the Lord of Holdernesse's son and who killed the school's German master. And you say that the gallows await this man who was both kidnapper and killer."

"Your recollection of my comment at the time is accurate," said Holmes, who, unusually, appeared at first unsure as to how to respond.

"Yet the kidnapping was carried out on the instigation of the Lord of Holdernesse's own natural son, James Wilder. You acquiesce in that."

"I must commend you for your attention to the detail of the case. For me, one case seems to merge into another, particularly at this distance of time."

"So, in fact, you allow your silence on the true brains behind the plot to be bought for £12,000 and retire from professional services thereafter."

"I thought a penalty of £12,000 from his lordship an ample punishment for him and a suitable reward to me for finding his legitimate son. I could see no point in doing anything about the flight of his natural son. And by 1903, I felt I had done as much as I could in criminal work and was anxious to focus my attention on other fields."

"So, you permitted his well-to-do illegitimate son to escape the consequence of his crime. And allowed another poorer man to hang for it. So, you benefitted personally from a crime. And yet you say in *The Final Problem* that in over a thousand cases, you have never knowingly used your powers on the wrong side. When I read those words, Mr Holmes, tears came into my eyes as I felt at one with you in my desire to bring about world revolution. But in the case of *The Priory School*, I cannot see you have used your powers on the right side for that and another man has had to hang to pay for your retirement."

He paused.

"I thought you were a revolutionary hero, but I find, Mr Holmes, that you have feet of clay. Have you been paid to bring me your message of an attack on my country? I no longer think that these quarters at the Hotel Metropol are suitable for a traitor to the revolution, and I must accommodate you somewhere which you may perhaps find rather less prepossessing."

Holmes remained calm.

"A case from nearly forty years ago cannot possibly be of significance to us now. I would remind the General Secretary that I recorded train movements in Germany consistent with a colossal movement of people and material. The magnitude was such as to exclude the possibility that it was anything other than a military build-up, and the direction of travel left no doubt as to which country would be the target of the military action. Once you have excluded the impossible, whatever remains, no matter how improbable, must be true. And a German invasion of the Soviet Union can hardly be described as improbable. I have taken huge risks to come to Moscow to tell you about it. And my friend has too."

"You may exclude the impossible to your heart's content, Mr Holmes, but here we are, a month later and the Germans are still on the other side of the border. They are short of metals, oil, and grain. All of these they get from us without doing more than paying us and, even then, not always in cash. We even sell them rubber from British India which they have no other means of getting for themselves. And which they would certainly not get at all if we were at war with them."

"Then, General Secretary, they are using material with which you provided them to launch an attack on you."

"You and your friend will hang if there is no invasion," Stalin burst out at this undiplomatic reproof to his judgement.

The soldier said, "Pack and follow me."

We had not brought more than the clothes we stood up in from Berlin and, although the Hotel Metropol had been able to supply us with a few desiderata, it was not long before we had left its comfort and were entering the forbidding precincts of what we were to learn was Lefortovo prison.

In the adventure of the *Bruce-Partington Plans* which had taken place nearly half a century earlier in 1895, Lestrade had said that one day Holmes and I would go too far in our investigations and that we would find ourselves in trouble. It is hard to overstate how much trouble we were in here – in prison in a country run by a savage dictator and our whereabouts known to no one who might be in any sort of position to help us.

The only comfort we were offered was the fact we were allocated a cell with bunk beds together.

In 1895, Holmes's response to Lestrade's foreboding had been a cheery comment to me, "For England, home, and beauty – eh, Watson? Martyrs on the altar of our country."

Then, the prospect of becoming a martyr for my country had been a remote one, although Holmes's cavalier attitude towards it had disturbed me even in 1895. Now, imprisoned in a fortress which was notorious for having been where victims of the Great Purge of 1937 had met their fates, I was unable to avoid falling into the deepest depression. It was not that we were badly treated ourselves, but it was the regular reports from massed gunfire and the cries of anguish – I assume from other prisoners although we never saw anyone apart from our guards – that echoed down the corridors, and which made our time so difficult to bear. A few books in English were made available to us, but I was unable to focus on anything in our gloomy cell. Holmes, by contrast, found among the books a Russian grammar book and dictionary, and he spent hours going through them.

"I have always said, good Watson, that one should keep in one's attic of knowledge only those things which might be useful to one. Who knows what use I might be able to make of knowledge of Russian?"

"It would certainly be of use if you were able to ask our executioner to make sure he has available a rope of sufficient length to ensure us a mercifully swift end," I commented, gallows humour taking on a clear and pressing meaning for me.

But Holmes, engrossed in his studies of Russian, bestowed no further words on me.

The days merged into each other and the nights, as mid-summer's night day approached, were short indeed, although from our barred window we could see the utter blackness in the small hours of the night that we had seen in London and Berlin. It was in the twilight very late on the night of the 21st of June before he spoke again.

"I would rather be here at the nexus of world events than anywhere else. Indeed, I would not swap our current situation even to step back to Baker Street and my halcyon days as my biographer made me famous," he said at last, his voice infused with the spirit he always showed when on a case.

"And you regard being in a cell in a notorious prison as being at the nexus of world affairs." I riposted.

There was a silence.

"If the Germans," I continued, "do not launch an invasion soon, this case may actually prove to be our final problem," the thought occurring to me that documenting our adventure – apparently the latest in every sense – might make time pass more easily. "Perhaps you would tell me about the results of your investigations in Berlin."

"I have said to you before, that an event without features is far harder to unravel than one with a motivation. The cases of mine which you have been kind enough to chronicle have all had a motivation even if – as in the case of the apparently random destruction of the six busts of Napoleon - that motivation was not immediately obvious. In that case, the identification of the motivation made the resolution of the case fairly straightforward. In the case of the S-Bahn killer, the victims had nothing more to do with one other than that they lived in a large city and were obliged to use the S-Bahn or main overground train system."

"So, what was your *modus operandi* for the case?"

"The only unifying feature was the killer, and I knew I would have to find a way to identify him. The only way I could hope to do that was to note some unique feature about him."

"How could you hope to do that?"

"I made my preparation in the gramophone room of the Adlon Hotel?"

"I saw you in there, but you gave no sign of seeing me. And how would that help you in noting a feature of the S-Bahn killer."

"I was aware you had seen me. I fear, good Watson, that whereas I could say with justice to people they should expect to see no trace of me when

I trailed them, the smell of the smoke from your Bradley's of Oxford Street cigarette brought back happy memories to me of Baker Street when you trailed me to the gramophone room of the Adlon Hotel and observed me bowed over the gramophone there."

"So, you did see me there but gave no sign of it?"

"On the contrary Watson, while I knew you were within twenty paces of me, my focus was on improving my eye-sight."

"Improving your eye-sight? And yet you could not see me?"

"The eye is a muscle that is capable of strengthening like any other. What I was employing is a technique I have heard of sportsmen using. They write letters of the alphabet at random onto a piece of paper and try to pick them out as they spin round the turntable of a gramophone."

"Your method does not seem to have worked if you could not see me across a dimly lit room."

"It was rather like learning to play my violin showpieces on three strings, good Watson. Once the fourth string was restored, playing the pieces on four strings immediately seemed much easier. I had taken the opportunity to make seeing more difficult in a dim room by taking laudanum before I went down. The good Obermann had provided me with it, just as he had provided you with your Bradley of Oxford Street cigarettes. Laudanum is an opiate that reduces the pupils to pinholes and that is I suspect what they looked like when you saw me."

"But how then were you able to identify me by sight in the air-raid shelter only an hour or so later."

"The Pervitin."

"The Pervitin?"

"The pills that Madson had, were a cocaine-based stimulant which widens the pupils. A cocaine-based stimulant is another of the pleasures of Baker Street I had not partaken of for many a year," said Holmes with a sigh, "and Obermann was able to furnish me with a goodly supply of it. I took the pills immediately after I had completed the exercise with the gramophone record. Pervitin widens the pupils so that one is more capable of seeing in darkness. So, having made things more difficult for my eyes by smoking laudanum, I stimulated the muscles in the exercise with the gramophone. And then having taken Pervitin, I was able to see you in that dimmest light of the Adlon's air-raid shelter."

"So, you believe Madson's theory that it was the use of Pervitin that enabled the Germans to beat two superior armies last year?"

"I am sure that it helped but that is not relevant to the matter at hand. I knew that to capture a killer operating at random on a train, my best chance was to see him, note some feature that identified him, and then to use that feature to track him down. I am certainly sure my experiments with laudanum and Pervitin enabled me to identify you in the air-raid shelter of the Adlon Hotel and to spot the handbag in the bush beside the railway line for the last victim whose body we saw."

"But none of the killer's surviving victims had spotted anything special about their attacker. And nor did Lüdtke, Brunner, or I when we glimpsed the killer jumping from the train."

"The victims were taken by surprise and had no reason to take the measures I had done to improve their night vision. And the police had not thought to do so. Lüdtke and Nebe are like Gregson and Lestrade in their failure to use their imagination."

"So, what did you see when you saw Brunner's attacker?"

"With my pupils dilated with Pervitin, I was able to see he had a broken nose and a disproportionately flared right nostril probably caused by the trauma that had broken his nose."

"And what was your next move?"

"I was unable to make my next move as we returned to our hotel to find that we had been summoned back to London. Having received the summons, I could be sure we were not seeking to have more prisoners-of-war released so I was constrained from giving Lüdtke any advice on the continued conduct of the case."

"And that is why you sought to look through personnel records?"

There was a pause.

"That is so."

There was something odd about Holmes's account of his *modus operandi,* but I was not sure how to formulate it without accusing him of lying.

In the end, as I thought of the execution pit next door, I felt I had no choice.

"So, what was the precise nature of the summons to the Foreign Office to which I was not invited? And why your lack of interest in the prisoners-of-war on our second sojourn in Berlin? And why, having got your clue, which should have rendered your search for the criminal relatively straightforward, have you not at least organized an identity parade?"

Silence in the darkness.

"I believe," I said at length, and, at last questioning Holmes's judgment made our cell feel clothed in half-light rather than half-darkness, "that you were sent by the Foreign Office, not to investigate the crime, but to spy on Germany's plans."

Silence.

"And that you needed my presence to make your presence plausible. So, I was your alibi for what you were doing."

Silence.

"And that if your true motives had become known to the Germans, we would both have been hanged as spies. And, if the Germans do not launch an invasion soon, that will be our fate here as well."

"It is a principle of British law," came back the answer, "that silence cannot be taken to indicate anything."

"There must have been some new policy, some new source of advice at the Foreign Office that had us go back to Berlin....."

My insights were interrupted by the sound of a rattle of keys, and our cell door opened.

Stalin entered with an interpreter. A screen was put over our window and we were soon blinking as a light was lit.

"And here, Mr Holmes," said Stalin, through the interpreter who entered our cell with him, "unless I am very much mistaken, is someone who has no need to be your next client."

He paused to laugh at his own joke.

"I am very sorry for this inconvenience to you gentlemen," he continued, "but I fear I will not be in a position to know what to do with you for a few days yet. Napoleon chose the 24th of June 1812 as the day to invade us, and he ran out of time before our winter took hold. I will decide what to do with you once that deadline is past. I could ransom you," he said casually, and knocked out his pipe against the bars across our window. "Or I could use you as a demonstration of what happens to spies and spreaders of misinformation in our country. And to enemies of the people in the global class struggle."

There seemed nothing further to say and a silence hung in the air which was interrupted by a frantic banging on the door of our cell.

Stalin barked a curse and disappeared out into the corridor.

I heard an exchange, but I speak no Russian although I could hear something that sounded like "Nemet" which meant nothing to me. I also heard the word "Liskow" and wondered if this was the name of a Russian town.

When Stalin came back into our cell he was quite bereft of his previous swagger.

Our interpreter had stayed in our cell with us during the Soviet leader's absence, and Holmes turned to him and said, "Could you ask the General Secretary at what time Private Liskow said the German attack would take place when he swam across the River Bug?"

As the interpreter was translating to Stalin, Holmes turned to me and said, "I would not have known that 'Nemet' is the Russian for German without my study of the Russian dictionary. And I deduced the rest. So, my time in this cell has not been totally in vain. Even if we do still end up getting hanged."

The Soviet leader ground out an answer which the interpreter translated as, "Three o'clock in the morning. A German deserter swam the river to say that an attack was imminent."

"Private Liskow is obviously somebody else whose diplomacy is not insincere. He has taken huge risks to bring the news of the impending invasion," observed Holmes mildly, and the interpreter conveyed his comment to Stalin. "As did Dr Watson and I. Before you incarcerated us."

Stalin glared, and then asked almost plaintively.

"Have you told anyone else of what Hitler is planning?"

"The only people to whom I have spoken about it, are present in this cell."

"Will the British join me in a fight against my invader?"

"General Secretary, the British have waged war against the Hitler for nearly two years. We have nothing to show for that struggle and yet we continue with it. I suspect that if Hitler were to invade hell, Mr Churchill would at least make a friendly reference to the devil in the House of Commons."

Stalin lit his pipe.

"We will need an alliance. The British and the Russians fought together against Napoleon in the first half of the last century and together we can defeat Hitler in the first half of this one. I think we must find a way to make the British see that this is also in their interest to have a deal."

He stood in thought and then his face cleared.

"I think I have a way to make them understand the urgency of the situation. It may not look like it tomorrow morning, but we Soviets are used to winning wars in the end. If the British want my help, they must agree to my terms. They must recognise my present western frontier with Germany as my final western frontier."

"But," objected Holmes, "you seized that from Poland in your pact with Hitler."

"As I indicated to you before, we restored our western frontier, and we want to keep it that way. And when we win this war, the British must allocate to my sphere of influence, everywhere where my armies stop west of our present frontier. That will mean that any future European conflict will take place well to the west of us."

"But, General Secretary," objected Holmes again, "the Germans are about to invade you and you are already redrawing the map of Europe."

"The future belongs, Mr Holmes, to those who plan for it, not to those who wish for a different present. And he who controls the present, controls the future. And, since the British look to be in no hurry to stage a landing in France, I want them to send me all their excess industrial production."

"And what will you offer in return?"

"I will fight. I may not be blessed with the powers of oratory of your Mr Churchill, but we will fight the Germans everywhere we find them. To the last bullet. Our armies will soon find that it is less dangerous to advance than to retreat. And we will not offer the Germans a separate peace."

"And how will I get back to London to negotiate this, General Secretary?"

"I do not see a role for you in negotiating this, Mr Holmes."

"Then how do you propose to negotiate it at all?"

Stalin turned to me.

"Somewhat at variance to the normal course of events in your accounts of your friend's work, Dr Watson, I am commissioning you to negotiate this."

"You want me to negotiate this?" I gasped.

"I think the presence of you, Dr Watson, in London with the knowledge that Mr Sherlock Holmes is languishing in a cell in Moscow next door to a gallows will focus the minds of your political masters."

"You think that the judgment of the British government might be swayed by the fate of an eighty-seven-year-old man?" objected Holmes, presenting Stalin's proposal as a piece of logic that needed pressure-testing, and, I think, indifferent to his own fate for all that I could see myself sharing it.

"I think British morale, Mr Holmes," replied Stalin through his interpreter, "might take something of a blow if it were known that a symbol of all that is good old England had been in Berlin on a mission, the nature of which he will not disclose."

He paused and puffed at his pipe.

"And I think that the man of words in your partnership, Mr Holmes, is Dr Watson rather than you. I have taken the opportunity to read the two late adventures, *The Blanched Soldier*, set after the end of the Boer War in 1901 but undated, and *The Lion's Mane,* set in your ill-gotten retirement, in which you are the narrator. If I am blunt, I find them far less persuasive than the works from Dr Watson's pen. So, I think Dr Watson is the man to perform the negotiations, while your presence here will focus minds in London."

Flight and Traps

I was on a train from Moscow to Leningrad at midnight and at nine o'clock in the morning local time I was at an air-strip for a flight to Stockholm.

I could only follow gestures since no one with whom I came into contact, spoke any English and, as I followed my pilot to a fighter 'plane, I noted other fighters parked in neat lines on the turf. We taxied out and then accelerated towards take-off.

As our wheels left the ground to head west, heading east towards us came what I knew to be German fighters. My pilot made a sound which I assume was a curse and, as we soared upwards, I looked back and saw most of the 'planes that had been parked so neatly beside the runway had been set ablaze.

To my horror my pilot turned round and pursued the attackers, but his craft was too unwieldy to make a proper sally, and the enemy was soon disappearing out of sight, although he fired his gun until the magazine clicked to indicate he had exhausted his ammunition.

We turned west once more, and I saw another wave of German fighters and bombers heading east which meant that our 'plane could not be outpaced although we were now unarmed. My heart was in my mouth as my pilot headed straight into their squadron as though seeking a collision. If we had been more than a single 'plane, I suspect the black-crossed enemy craft would have taken on the challenge but, as it was, they swerved out of the way, and continued on their way to their bombing mission.

If I had any illusions that the Germans might conceivably not be at war with the Soviets, they were gone now. The assault was on, and no preparations had been made to thwart attacks on Soviet 'planes on the ground by parking them irregularly as we had had to learn the previous year in what is now known as the Battle of Britain.

And if I had any doubts now about the Soviets' willingness to fight to the last man, the actions of my pilot had put them to rest as well.

It was perhaps fortunate that our flight, rather than being over land, was westwards across the Gulf of Finland, so no one else sought to attack us.

In Stockholm I was able to get the last seat on a 'plane which, like the flight from Bristol to Lisbon, I, and I suspect almost everybody in Britain, had never heard of. This was the so-called ball-bearing run – so named because ball-bearings were its main cargo – between the Swedish capital and Leuchars, near Fife in Scotland. As for our previous flights to

Portugal, we flew by night at an altitude which had us skimming the brine.

I sent a telegraph to the Foreign Office and was told to come down to London as soon as possible and present myself at 10 Downing Street.

From Leuchars I was able to get a taxi to Perth and from there the night express saw me at Downing Street on the morning of Tuesday the 24th of June 1941.

When I got to Downing Street, I would have expected to be taken to the Cabinet room, but instead was asked to go up to the Prime Minister's private flat which is in the floors above the state rooms on the ground floor. Its door was opened, to my surprise, by Oliver, the female auxiliary who had accompanied Holmes and me to Bristol in March, and I was taken to a private office.

I was soon joined by Mr Churchill himself along with Mr Eden, but my reader will be surprised by the identity of the third person in the welcoming party who was none other than an aged Mycroft Holmes (to whom I shall refer as Mycroft to avoid confusion with Sherlock Holmes). Mycroft was bowed with age, and no longer the portly figure of the last time I had seen him, but he was still endowed with that pair of grey eyes which bestowed his unmistakeable sense of mastery.

"It is hard," began Mycroft as though in self-explanation to me, "to give up the habits of a lifetime as *being* the British government, and, when Mr Churchill asked me to return to my role this spring, I could see no way of refusing."

"I am myself in my mid-sixties and can see no harm at all in drawing on the experiences of someone nearly thirty years older than myself. It is my view that the first method for estimating the intelligence of a ruler is to look at the calibre of the men he has around him although, as with all advisors, I see the role of Mr Mycroft Holmes to be on tap but not on top," said Mr Churchill, waving an inevitable cigar breezily around, before taking a nip of what looked like a glass of weak cold tea at his right hand.

I laid out to Churchill, Eden, and Mycroft what Stalin had proposed and laid particular emphasis on the fate of my friend if the General Secretary's terms were not met.

"But we went to war for Poland," objected Eden, as the implications of Stalin's demands sank in. "We will be betraying our Polish allies if we accept this. It cannot be honourable to accept the final destruction of a vanquished ally to appease a potential new ally who until three days ago was in a pact with our enemy. If the Soviets win against the Germans, they will have been rewarded for their aggression against the Poles."

"And if the Germans win, they will be rewarded for their aggression against everyone," responded Mycroft.

Mr Churchill asked that a map of Europe be brought before us, and we were soon all four standing before us as it hung from the wall.

"So, if we say the Soviets can have all this," mused the Prime Minister at last, pointing with his cigar at where it was now proposed the Soviet Union should be, "although of course they occupy it anyway, they will undertake to fight to the last man."

"They will fight to the last man in any circumstance," growled Eden. "They have been invaded."

"All our allies have said they would fight to the last man against the German enemy after they were attacked, yet I do not recall any other country that has not, in the end, made terms with their German

212

invader," rejoindered Churchill. "The Poles, the Danes, the Norwegians, the Belgians, the Dutch, the Luxembourgers, the French, the Yugoslavs, and the Greeks. All committed themselves to that. And all ended up signing an instrument of surrender. Here we have an ally who has a huge territory and a huge army. We would be failing in our duty to prosecute the war if we do not help the Soviets in any way we can."

"But what is proposed will leave Poland partitioned with part of it within the Soviet Union and a rump state which will be wedged between Germany and the Soviet Union. It will barely be viable."

"The Poles can have some German territory," rejoindered Churchill with a shrug. "That is what happens after a country loses a war. There is East Prussia and these towns here," he said, waving his cigar vaguely in the general direction of Stettin and Danzig on the Baltic seaboard, and Breslau inland.

"But that will mean the need to move millions of people from those parts of Poland that will become Soviet into the new boundaries of Poland as well as moving millions of Germans out of East Prussia and what is now Poland into some new German state."

"This first half of the twentieth century has seen one forced population move after another. The Greeks and the Turks have swapped populations, the Germans have been forced out of the Alsace and parts of Eastern Europe, and the Protestants out of Southern Ireland." Churchill shrugged again. "And the alternative is to have a minority population of permanent malcontents – and you saw how far that got us with the remaining Germans in the Sudetenland and in Poland. What is proposed is perhaps the worst possible solution. Apart from all the others that might be tried."

"But if they win, the Soviets have said they will want under their sphere of influence any land controlled by their army to the west of their new border. We have no means at present to make a landing in Western Europe, so that means that they could, theoretically control all of Western Europe to the Atlantic."

"Are you suggesting a more palatable alternative, Foreign Secretary? Let us consider the possible outcomes. If the Germans win against the Soviets, they will recoil upon us, with renewed vigour, strengthened by an empire that will stretch from the Urals to the Bay of Biscay. But if the Soviets push the Germans back, well," he paused and drew on his cigar, "we will need to have made some advances against the Germans from the west to prevent the Soviets from achieving dominion over the whole of Europe, but the Germans will be fighting a war on two fronts, and so staging a landing in Western Europe and securing land there should be within the capabilities of our land forces. And while the main fault-line in Europe where conflicts arise is at present on the French German border, it will then be well to the east of there that Europe's main fault-line lies."

"Maybe if we and the Soviets are the dominant powers in Europe," interjected Mycroft Holmes, "and the status of the Germans and the French as great powers is correspondingly diminished, those two nations might even find an equitable way of sharing the coal and iron deposits that straddle their borders, and which have caused so much conflict between them in the past. It is an arrangement other nations on Western Europe might also want to partake of."

Mr Churchill gave Mycroft a glance, "Maybe so, but we are getting ahead of ourselves, and such an arrangement is one that this country would, in any case, be far too important to involve itself in. This country will always be directing its ambitions and energies well beyond the confines of the European continent."

"But we are exchanging a German-dominated Eastern Europe for one dominated by the Soviets," objected Eden.

"We can insist that in those territories they conquer, the Soviets hold elections which will diminish their influence in their sphere. I do not believe that Poles will vote for politicians in the pocket of the Soviets."

"And Poland is losing a hundred miles of territory to its east," protested Eden.

"But that is all unhospitable marshland. And it will be gaining prosperous cities to its west. The Poles will have a fine new country three to four-hundred miles square and with two-hundred and fifty miles of Baltic coastline rather than a narrow Polish corridor to the sea. They would be fools not to accept these proposals."

"And are we to accept Soviet political hegemony over Southern Europe as well as over Eastern Europe?"

"With our own troops already in Northern Africa, we will be in more of a position to shape events in Southern Europe then we are in Eastern Europe. Perhaps we could formalise arrangements by offering the Soviets 90% of the influence over Poland in exchange for us having 90% of the influence in Greece."

So it was, that the map of Europe was carved up in Churchill's office on the afternoon of the 24th of June 1941. I commented to Mr Churchill that if the war ended with Europe having the spheres of influence he envisaged, then a curtain of iron would fall on a line from Stettin at the Baltic shore to Trieste in the Adriatic.

He shrugged and in the end said, "Your command of language has never been in any doubt, Dr Watson. The difficulty is to achieve these ends to which we strive. An iron curtain from Stettin to Trieste would be well to the east of where the main causes of European tensions had been before the German attack on the Soviets. And the chances of achieving such a settlement are certainly better now than anything that might have been conceivable even a week ago."

For my own part I found the process I had just seen completely unreal.

The news from the German-Soviet war that I had been able to read in a newspaper on the way down from Perth had been uniformly catastrophic, and updates brought in during our meeting only confirmed the picture. In less than two days, the Germans had advanced one-hundred miles into territory previously controlled by the Soviets and they were laying siege to Brest-Litovsk, which I had passed through on my way to Moscow only a few weeks previously.

"If we are fortunate, those territories will become part of the Soviet Union whose authority over them we will then be compelled to recognise," mused Mycroft. "And if we are unfortunate, the situation will be even worse."

"And what about the fate of your brother?" I asked Mycroft.

"Oh yes," said my friend's brother in a distracted manner. "I had almost forgotten about him. When I gave him his brief and suggested that your presence would provide a good cover for it, I did think young Sherlock might get rather out of his depth, and so it has proved. Well, I suppose it is in no one's interests that my brother should be hanged. We should add his immediate release to the list of conditions that we insist on before we agree to give the Soviets any help. His death would be a tragedy although we are here looking at deaths in millions for which there is no scope for individual pity."

With the outcome of our discussions settled very much on the terms Stalin had specified, I was soon back on the ball-bearing run to Stockholm and thence via a fighter 'plane back to Moscow. As I was driven to the Kremlin, I saw that I had arrived at a city transformed from what I had seen previously. Just as London bristled with pill-boxes for a land-assault and air-raid shelters against air-attacks, so now I saw women in bright head-scarves labouring in the summer heat to construct fortifications of all sorts on Moscow's streets as I was driven from the station to the Kremlin.

"So, what does your government say?" asked Stalin through his interpreter at my arrival.

"We can accept your terms. We will recognise your western borders as they stood last Saturday, we will not make a separate peace with Germany, and we will provide you with any war production not essential to our own efforts. But," I added cautiously, and this was what I feared might be the sticking point in our discussions, "we must insist on elections in any territory you conquer west of those borders which we will now undertake to recognise."

I confess my heart was beating as I waited for this condition to be translated to Stalin. I feared the whole agreement might unravel over it as I thought it was obvious that the Poles would not vote in an election for a government that would be palatable to Stalin after his troops had invaded that country less than two years before. But the Soviet leader shrugged and gave an airy wave of his pipe while his interpreter translated his words back to me.

"Of-course I have no wish to coerce any people who does not wish to adhere to us for whatever reason. Although in the elections that we organise in those territories to the west of our borders which, as I predicted, your government has now recognised, it might perhaps be slightly less important whom the people choose and," he paused, considering his words, "perhaps slightly more important who counts the votes....."

"And we must insist on the immediate release of my friend, Sherlock Holmes."

".... And I have an idea on how we can save ourselves some work on drafting the treaties," Stalin added brightly, ignoring my comment. "We can take our existing treaty with the Germans and replace the word Germany with Great Britain. The terms of what you have agreed to here are all pretty much the same as what we had previously agreed with them, and I see no reason to give our legal drafters any more work than is necessary. We need all the manpower we can get at the front."

This comment on the terms agreed was no more than the truth – actually, although his new enemy was advancing with alarming speed, Stalin had a better deal from us than he had had from the Germans, as our supplies to him would be on a *pro bono* basis.

I repeated my demand for the release of Holmes and the dictator shrugged.

"Well, I suppose if I let the mouthpiece of a traitor to the class struggle go to negotiate for me in London, and he has delivered me the deal I was looking for, I suppose equally that there is no reason why I should not now let the traitor himself go. It makes no difference to me."

"And how will we get back to London?"

"That too will be arranged."

While transport was organised, we found ourselves back at the Hotel Metropol.

This time we were allowed more freedom to move within the hotel, and one of our fellow guests was Graf Friedrich-Werner von der Schulenburg, the aged German ambassador to the Soviet Union, whose job it has been to deliver the declaration of war to Molotov, the Soviet Foreign Secretary, on that fateful morning of the 22nd of June. Von der Schulenburg recognised us and the Soviets, I suspect because they had planted listening devices in the hope of learning something if we spoke to von der Schulenburg, made no attempt to prevent discussions.

"For the last six years I have personally tried to do everything I could to encourage friendship between the Soviet Union and Germany. I warned our people of the difficulties an invasion would cause us, and I warned the Soviets of my suspicions of German intentions, but they dismissed what I said it as British duplicity. God knows how I'll get home now if I get home at all. And it all comes down to that Austrian corporal who has no experience of anything."

But within a few days he had been swapped for his opposite number in Berlin while Holmes and I were transported back to Britain, arriving on the 1st of July. When we arrived from Stockholm at Leuchars, we were told we were to be taken to an unknown location yet, as we headed south down the Great North Road, we seemed to be headed only for Fenny Stratford. But although we passed within a few hundred yards of our cottage, our car continued on its way.

"We are going to Chequers," said Holmes. "Nowhere else makes sense. It is only twenty miles from our cottage, I imagine the Prime Minister spends a lot of time at his country home there to avoid the bombs in London. But as far as I can see, our role in this matter is at an end. What more is there for us to discuss?"

Woman-Officer Oliver opened the door for us – in wartime even Chequers appeared unable to run to a butler – and she ushered us into a room where Churchill and Mycroft were seated.

"We will," said Churchill, "shortly be joined by the American ambassador, and we are going to try, not for the first time, to persuade him to intercede for us with President Roosevelt so that the United States joins us in a formal military alliance. The United

States has declined to join us so far, but it may be the latest developments, of which you have first-hand knowledge, are what we need to move forward."

I heard what sounded like a friendly exchange between Oliver and Winant at the door before the latter entered.

"I am happy to say," said Churchill, "that we have agreed terms for an alliance in our struggle against Germany with the Soviet Union. I hope that will convince your President to throw his lot in with us."

"I am not aware that we had ever sought to be in an alliance with the Bolsheviks," responded Winant.

"In pursuit of victory over our foe, we cannot afford to be too choosy about who might be our bedfellows. We are fighting for the preservation of civilisation in this continent."

"And you are asking for us to join you in the fight in that continent, even though it is over two thousand miles from our shores, even though you admit to having no means of driving back your enemies on land yourselves, and even though we are ourselves menaced by the Japanese."

"I am sure you can persuade your President that, through no fault of its own, this country is incapable of staging a landing on Continental Europe, and that it is not in the interests of the United States for the continent of Europe to be under the thumb of either the Germans or the Soviets which is what will happen if the United States do not bring their boundless resources to bear on this conflict."

"Great Britain has an empire which spans the globe. You yourself have speculated that it might last a thousand years. We are already supporting you in your struggle against the Axis powers with war materials. It will be hard to persuade my countrymen to risk their lives in a European conflict, especially when we sent men to Europe only just over twenty years ago."

"I thought you said, Mr Winant," interjected I, turning to my friend Sherlock Holmes for his support, "when we greeted you on your arrival at Bristol, that your President will take account in his actions of what you say, so if you are convinced by our need for direct American support, so will he be."

"So he will, so he will. But what I said to you and Mr Holmes then was diplomacy. There are all the objections I have outlined to acting on what you are proposing. And American public opinion is solidly against our becoming more involved than we are already."

Discussions continued along these lines until nearly nine o'clock and Churchill asked Winant to stay for what he said would be an exceedingly modest dinner, "Although, however paltry our food rations," added the Prime Minster, shaking the pale brown liquid in his glass thoughtfully, "we are unlikely to suffer from thirst. You may prefer to spend the night here as well, rather than returning to London."

Winant assented and was taken up to his room.

When he had gone, Mycroft murmured, "To get a fair wind to Troy, Agamemnon sacrificed his daughter, Iphigenia, to obtain the favour of the goddess Artemis."

"I am reassured," replied Churchill, "that we will not need to go quite as far as that. Our trans-Atlantic cousins always do the right thing in the end, although they do, I confess, always explore every other option first."

"Winant had had his boots resoled," commented Holmes, apropos nothing in particular. "I noted that when I met him on his arrival from Iceland."

"I, of course, also noted that at my first encounter with him," retorted Mycroft loftily, "and I drew the same rather obvious inference about Mr Winant's financial means that you drew about Lord Holdhurst in *The Naval Treaty*. I also noted that Mr Winant arrived without his wife." There was a pause before Mycroft continued, "And now, good Sherlock, I fear I see no further role for you in this matter. I have ordered you a car to take you home."

Holmes looked nonplussed by the turn of events, but it was clear from Mycroft's demeanour that this was an instruction rather than an invitation for Holmes to leave. I was even more nonplussed to realise that Mycroft was expecting me to stay.

"I recall that in *The Dying Detective*, Dr Watson," said Mycroft to me, after his brother had gone, "you concealed yourself much as you did only a few short weeks ago on the train from Berlin to Moscow. Such concealment is obviously something for which you have a talent, however slighting my brother is about your abilities. You and I will have a light supper in the kitchen while the Prime Minister and Mr Winant dine *tête-à-tête*."

It was over our supper that Mycroft told me his plan and just before ten I concealed myself in the space behind the bedhead in Winant's room.

Fortunately, my vigil there was not very long.

Winant came up and retired and soon afterwards that there was a discreet knock on the door. The American diplomat rose, and I heard a murmur of conversation at the door. His interlocutor was Woman-Officer Oliver.

My more adult readers will need no insight from me on what happened next, and I will confine myself to the remark that I rapidly found my hiding place behind the bedhead rendered hazardous.

But suddenly, the bedroom door was thrown open, the light came on, and Mycroft entered.

"I am most reluctant to disturb the ambassador," said he, "but he must realise that his assignation with the Prime Minister's daughter may not be seen in a favourable light by his President. Some people are so unwilling to display any understanding of the travails of an international lifestyle."

"You have no witnesses. It will be your word against mine," replied the American diplomat, while Miss Churchill egressed with a blinding swiftness.

"There, Ambassador, I think, you may be mistaken. Dr Watson, would you mind emerging from your hiding place."

Winant looked aghast as I emerged from behind his bed.

"Dr Watson, Mr Winant," purred, Mycroft, "is a man whose record of integrity is unimpeachable. That is why he was the person sent to greet you at Whitchurch Airport. And his word will be believed in a way that no one else's will, should he be prevailed upon to report on what he has witnessed this evening. And his patriotism will tell him that he has no choice but to report on what he has seen if he is instructed to do so."

"A honey-trap!" exclaimed Winant.

"I have no choice but to concur that your judgment may be called into come into question if what has happened here tonight becomes public knowledge. But you may like to reflect that if this matter remains secret, you will be able to carry on enjoying the company of the delightful Miss

Churchill, so you have both a positive and a negative reason for falling in with our wishes."

"What do you want?"

"I would have thought that what we want should be clear to you. We want your advocacy of your American support on our side in Europe. We need you to urge your President that we are the people whom he must back with war-material and troops. And you must stress the sacrifices that people are making here in pursuit of victory. I am sure Dr Watson here will help you so to craft the wording of your despatches, that their plangency has the maximum impact with the President."

"But I have already said, our western coast is menaced by the Japanese, and that is likely to take priority amongst American concerns."

"Then you must advocate a policy of 'Europe first,' Ambassador. The closest the Japanese might get to you is thousands of miles from your mainland. If either the Germans or the Soviets achieve a decisive victory, it will be hard to see the contagion being kept from our shores. You would not wish your oldest ally to be plunged into the abyss of a new dark age, and its ability to act circumscribed by the baleful presence of either the National Socialists or the Bolsheviks in France."

A look at the face of Winant told me that Mycroft had got the backing for the cause that he wanted, and he and I progressed downstairs.

"When you catch them in the place where we caught Mr Winant, good Doctor," observed Mycroft serenely on the stair-case, "their hearts and minds soon follow. A good-looking married man dependent on the wealth of his wife is always susceptible. And the Prime Minister's daughter is an accomplished actress who played her role tonight to perfection. It is indeed a fortunate combination of events that she is at present estranged from her husband, Mr Oliver."

We were already on the gravelled drive and Mycroft continued.

"And here is the car to take you back to Fenny Stratford. It is a shame that you should have subtitled *His Last Bow* as Sherlock Holmes's wartime service for his work at the outbreak of the last war but will be unable to write a similar work now in celebration of the role you have played in the events tonight. It is hard indeed to imagine anyone playing any better."

By the 12th of July, the United Kingdom and the Soviet Union had signed a treaty of which the published text confined itself to both sides, ruling out a separate peace with Germany and offering each other mutual support, but to which I knew there were secret protocols covering the future boundaries of Eastern Europe and the respective spheres of influence of the parties. Meanwhile in August 1941, the United States and Great Britain signed the Atlantic Charter. And when in December 1941, the Japanese attacked Pearl Harbour, the British declared war on the Japanese several hours before the Americans did and, when Germany declared war on the Americans, the latter undertook to focus on the European theatre of war before that in the Far East, a promise that they acted on faithfully.

A Summer with the Newspapers

After the adventures of the early summer, we followed the next developments keenly but not from close at hand.

Wodehouse, whom Holmes, with a callousness uncharacteristic of him, but perhaps justified by the imperative of telling the Soviets of the impending invasion, had sent out of the Adlon Hotel as a decoy, was persuaded to make his broadcasts to the United States on CBS. They were light in tone and made no attempt to paint a rosy picture of National Socialist Germany. But they caused outrage in Britain, and he has been declared *persona non grata sine die* here.

In August of 1941, Holmes was reading the 26th of July edition of the *Völkischer Beobachter*. Under the headline "Woman killer executed," it reported the capture, trial, and execution of one Paul Ogorzow, and I append the article in full below.

A danger to the women of Berlin, already worn with care as their menfolk defend the Fatherland at the front, has been eliminated.

In recent months there have been attacks on women travelling on the S-Bahn by night.

The attacker was clearly a railway worker.

To protect German women from this outrage, the Berlin Kriminalpolizei, under the direction, of Detective Wilhelm Lüdtke, undertook a major investigation involving the interviewing of thousands of railway workers.

One name that was mentioned in interviews over and over again was National Socialist Party member and auxiliary signalman Paul Ogorzow, who was reported as being regularly missing from duty at his post at the Rummelsburg signal-box.

Ogorzow was arrested on the 17th of July and blood was found on his uniform.

Eventually he confessed to eight counts of murder and six attempted murders. He blamed his attacks on madness brought on by the failure of a Jewish doctor to treat a personal medical complaint and asked to be taken to a psychiatric unit.

This plea did not convince his judges, he was stripped of his party membership, and executed by guillotine at Plötzensee gaol yesterday.

In these times of struggle, when our country is menaced by its enemies on all sides, criminal acts must be punished with the exemplary severity and swiftness, as has been demonstrated here."

Holmes chuckled.

"My researches amongst the personnel records of the Reichsbahn turned up the names of four members of staff who lived reasonably close to the stretch of the S-Bahn where the attacks were occurring, who were of the right age to be the man we glimpsed on the train, and whose medical tests at the beginning of their employment revealed a trauma to the nose. I am pleased to note that Ogorzow was one of the four. Many years ago, I commented to you that if you identify that your killer smoked a Lunkah cigar, you narrow your field of research. Even half a century later in an environment as alien from the London of the late 1880s as it is possible to be, that principle holds."

"What do you make of Lüdtke's technique of questioning thousands of railway staff?"

"Once he had failed to apprehend the killer through the use of officers in disguise on the train, I am not sure what other strategy there was available to him. He solved his case in the end, but he did not think to make the preparations that I made to ensure that I had the best chance to spot a distinguishing feature of the killer if he caught him on the train. Between the time we were forced to leave Belin in December last year and his arrest in mid-July, the S-Bahn killer committed three more murders. Better targeted work by Lüdtke might have avoided these."

Holmes lit his pipe before continuing

"What did Lüdtke say to us about himself? Three fairies promised Hitler that all Germans would be intelligent, honest, and National Socialists, but a fourth fairy came along and said that Germans would ever have only two of those three qualities, and Lüdtke was not sure whether he himself was any more than honest. I do think Lüdtke is honest, and, for all his party membership, he is no more than a National Socialist fellow traveller. His intellectual level is on a par with that of Inspector Gregson, and that explains the failure of Lüdtke's investigative tactics, relative to what I might have achieved had I had a free hand in the case."

"And how well does Lüdtke's aphorism sum up the other people we met?"

"It is only helpful up to a point. We met Goebbels, who was a convinced believer. I would not doubt his candour, his intelligence, nor yet his malevolence. Nebe clearly believed in the National Socialist cause but seemed to have little idea of how to conduct a case. He was far more interested in finding someone to blame than in solving a problem.

Von der Schulenburg was ineffectual as a diplomat but no National Socialist."

Holmes's observations about the difficulty of using the classification Lüdtke had given us was demonstrated in a most extraordinary way three years later.

Graf Schenk von Stauffenberg made an assassination attempt on Hitler in what became known as the 20th of July plot, and nearly succeeded in killing Hitler. That the former German ambassador to Moscow, von der Schulenburg, was among those involved did not surprise me. But also caught up in the drag-net of the plotters was Arthur Nebe. On the face of it, and I only saw either of them at close quarters for a short time, they seemed most unlikely to engage in a common purpose. Holmes speculated that Nebe felt that Hitler was not going far enough while von der Schulenburg, wanted to help organise an orderly capitulation. Both ended up being hanged at Plötzensee.

And yesterday the suicide was announced of former ambassador United States ambassador to this country, John Winant, in whose entrapment I played such a prominent and inglorious part.

In his suicide note, he mentioned that his affair with Miss Churchill had come to an end, that his wife was divorcing him, and that his money had run out. Mr Churchill has already announced that he will be sending a wreath of four dozen yellow roses. My reader may like to speculate on the complexity of his emotions at this time – I am not even sure he was aware until now of his married daughter's relationship with Mr Winant.

And for Winant himself, it was an inglorious end, and yet his role in convincing Roosevelt of the imperative of supporting our cause and prioritising the European theatre of operations even after the Japanese had attacked the United States in the Pacific, should not be underestimated.

Much of Continental Europe lies in rubble, millions of Poles – the nationality against whom Hitler aggressed first - have been expelled from lands now part of the Soviet Union, a similar fate has befallen Germans in lands where they had lived for generations, while Bolshevik governments have been imposed in the lands now controlled by Soviets. But the settlement of affairs in our western part of Europe is far more favourable to us than it would have been if either the Germans or the Soviets had achieved hegemony over the whole of Europe on their own.

There is much in this work about means and ends on which reader must form his own view, but I cannot doubt the desirability of the ends achieved for all that one may question the means that were used.

The Redacted Sherlock Holmes Series

Born a few hundred yards from Baker Street and living three miles from Wisteria Lodge, Orlando Pearson is the creator of The Redacted Sherlock Holmes series which has already appeared in print, ebook, and audio.

These works bury forever the notion that Sherlock Holmes might not have been a historic person as he jousts with his contemporaries and heroes of all ages. Would you like to see Sherlock Holmes come to the rescue of Queen Victoria, interrogate Heinrich Himmler, clear Macbeth of murder, unravel King Oedipus's complexities, or provide advice to the Almighty? Then Orlando's works are for you.

Orlando is about to publish a book of plays derived from his works which have been translated into German and Italian.

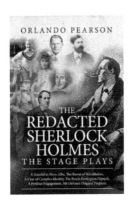

Kickstarter

A big thanks to all the backers in this book's Kickstarter campaign, and especially to those who asked for a mention in the book:

David Lars Chamberlain
Eric Sands
A Donaghey
Sergey Kochergan

Lightning Source UK Ltd.
Milton Keynes UK
UKHW020709071221
395242UK00013B/1616